What Happens in
the Highlands

What Happens in the Highlands

Kelsey McKnight

TULE
PUBLISHING

Chapter One

"**R**OSE HENSEL, PLEASE come to the baggage area. Rose Hensel to the baggage area," a woman's voice said in a professionally clipped accent over the loudspeaker.

Looking around at the myriad of signs that hung over other people's heads, I shouldered my heavy carry-on, feeling the straps dig in, and began pushing through the crowd. I had been wandering the terminal for some time, searching for somewhere to get a decent cup of coffee. But my search was in vain. While a seven-hour flight wasn't terrible to some people, I needed caffeine to survive and airplanes have the weakest brew of them all.

But now that someone was apparently searching for me, I had the renewed strength to continue on with my hike around the busy halls with a more concrete destination. Knowing my luck, I was being called because my bag had never arrived or had been searched by security and all my stuff was strewn all over the cargo hold of the plane and they needed me to identify my hairdryer on the tarmac.

The baggage claim was just as crowded as the rest of the airport with former passengers milling around, dragging luggage and small, cranky children behind them. I peered over the top of the carousels, trying to figure out exactly why I had been summoned and what I was supposed to do now that I was there. It hadn't been that long since I deplaned and it seemed like overkill for someone to page me over the intercom because I waited twenty minutes to pick up my single, large suitcase.

"Rosie!" a voice called out, reaching me at once.

I scanned the faces for the familiar one I knew was calling for me. It took less than a minute to find her bright orange curls bouncing around her face. She held a sign that said *Rosie Posey* in large glitter letters above her head and she jumped in excitement. While Scotland was the stereotypical land of the redheads, Katie Kazakov hardly blended in.

"Katie Cat!" I yelled in response, dropping my bag to the floor and throwing my arms around her neck as soon as I reached her.

She pulled back, looking me over. "I can't believe you're finally here!"

"And I can't believe you're getting married! Let me see the rock."

Katie held out her hand, showing me a sizable solitaire. "Sean says the diamond's from his great-grandmother's ring. Isn't that romantic?"

"Totally. But I got paged by... someone and—"

"Oh, that was me. When I didn't see you with the rest of the people around the New York City carousel, I kinda freaked a little. But I did get your suitcase already."

I looked around her. She didn't have any bags other than her own purse. "Where is it?"

"Oh, the driver put it in the car already." She waved a hand then hooked her arm through mine, pulling me towards the door. I hardly had time to grab my carry-on as we passed it.

"You have a driver?"

"Yeah. I'm getting the hang of driving on the other side of the road, but the traffic in Inverness is a little more than I'm used to in Nairn, so Sean had Mattie drive."

"Who's Mattie?"

"One of the garden guys or something." She looked around at the line of cars then pointed to a sleek black one parked by the sidewalk. "Here he is!"

Mattie was an older, stooped gentleman in khakis and a faded blue button-down. He had a pleasant, weathered face and smiled as they approached. "Miss Kazakov, Miss Hensel."

"Thank you for getting my bag," I said as he opened the back door for us. "Really, I could have gotten it."

"Do no' think of it, miss."

I shivered a bit when I was engulfed in the warm interior of the car and pulled out the sweater I kept in my carry-on bag, putting it on. "Katie, I thought it was supposed to be summer?"

"It *is* summer."

"Then why is it so cold?"

"Because it's Scotland," she said as if it were the perfect explanation.

I glanced at her thin, long-sleeve shirt and jeans. Not exactly like the June wardrobe we'd wear back in New Jersey. In my yoga pants and T-shirt, I felt particularly undressed for the weather. I knew it wasn't going to be the balmy temperature I was used to, but it was still a bit of a surprise.

"What does Sean do that he has a gardener and driver?" I asked in a hushed tone.

"Oh, Mattie's the family caretaker. He's in charge of making sure I stay out of trouble. Right, Mattie?"

"Aye, been workin' for the Calders goin' on forty years, I expect," he answered from the front seat as he pulled out into the line of traffic. "But Miss Kathryn really keeps me on my toes."

I was startled for a moment. For my entire life, she had been nothing but Katie to me. The only time I ever heard her referred to as Kathryn was on the first day of school when teachers would take roll. Only when we were too loud in the middle of the night during sleepovers or made a mess in the yard when we attempted to tie-dye our Backstreet Boys shirts did her parents ever call her Kathryn.

"Mattie's the best," Katie gushed. "He's really been a lifesaver when it came to me learning how to drive here. Sean was going to teach me, but he kept making me so nervous."

"Is it really hard to get used to being on the other side?" I asked.

"Ugh, I'll give you the full play-by-play on the horrors of left-side driving later." Katie smiled, her excitement bubbling over again. "I can't believe you're here. I'm so, so, *so* happy to see you."

"Same. I only wish Savannah could be here."

"Me, too. But I can't really blame her. She's a midwife, so it's not like she could just abandon her patients."

"I know. It just would have been really nice to see her, but I knew when I decided to get married so fast that some people couldn't come. I told her I'd send lots of pictures though when you got here, which reminds me..." she pulled out her cellphone and snapped a selfie of us together and sent it to our absent sorority sister and college best friend.

"It's been really quiet without you around. I've had to hang out with *other* people on the weekends since Savannah's always out delivery babies and putting on classes."

"You poor thing."

"But you're going to be a wife," I mused, looking out the windows at the passing city of Inverness.

It looked almost the same as any other in America, at least when it came to the tourists and people that milled around the busy streets. But the old stone buildings and steeple-topped churches told a different story. I could also see the tops of sailboats as we drove and wondered if fishing had been the thing to make the ancient village grow into a thriving city.

"I feel like it was just yesterday that we were going to kindergarten together, dorming together in college, and pledging a sorority... now you're getting *married*."

"I know, isn't it crazy? But you're going to love Sean. He's super sweet and so considerate and... you're just going to love him, Rose."

"If you love him, I'll love him. I just wish I could have made it over here before you got engaged and everything."

She shrugged and dragged her fingers through her curls. "It's not like I gave people much time. When I came here for work, I was only supposed to oversee the opening of a few stores, not meet a man and marry him in the span of three months."

"If he could woo you in less time than it takes for me to get a reservation at *George's* back home, I'm sure he's a catch."

"Trust me, he is. Something about the accent is just so swoon-worthy, right Mattie?"

Mattie glanced at her in the rearview mirror. "Oh, aye. Nothin' like a good touch o' Scot charm to turn the lass's heads."

"I do love a good accent," I sighed with my hands clasped, summoning my inner southern belle. "And I think the Scottish variety might be my favorite."

"Then you're in luck. I have plenty of single men on the guest list. Maybe you'll fall in love too and never leave."

"You're ridiculous."

"Come on, how great would that be? You'd marry one of Sean's friends or cousins and we'd all live happily ever after and be neighbors and raise our kids together and—"

"The only kind of romance I'm looking for is the kind that ends in the morning," I murmured, careful to not be overheard by Mattie. "I need to find out what a Scotsman wears under his kilt."

"Well, I can tell you that!"

"Hey, Sean's family now. That doesn't count." I peered back out the car window, looking to change the subject. "How long until we're at the hotel?"

"Only a half hour, thankfully. Was your flight okay?"

"Pretty nice, actually. I splurged on the first-class tickets."

"Cash in on all those airline miles?"

"Yeah. I haven't taken a vacation in six years since college. I needed to do *something* with them."

"Six years since college. We're so old."

"No, not that old… well, maybe you are, since you're about to get married."

She reached out, punching me jokingly on the arm, grimacing dramatically. "Hey, I am a glowing goddess of matrimonial bliss and you shall bow down at my altar."

We locked eyes for several moments, the only sound in the car was the faint rumble of street life outside. And then we burst into laughter, the kind that hurt our sides and made us tear up.

God, I was going to miss her.

THE LITTLE CITY of Nairn was just as adorable as I hoped. The stone-fronted houses gave it old-world charm that seemed to only be thriving still in the Scottish Highlands. The greys and greens that made up most of the area were inviting in a historic sense and I found myself only too excited to explore as soon as I found some spare time.

"And this is where my side of the wedding party will be staying," she said as Mattie stopped the car in front of a series of white buildings. The words *The Wild Thistle Hotel* were emblazoned over the double, purple doors. It looked like it was an old place, but as I entered the lobby, Katie behind me with my suitcase, I found it was surprisingly modern. There were scrubbed, hardwood floors, contemporary light fixtures, and the walls were painted a light lavender.

"Good afternoon, Miss Kazakov," a woman in a sharp suit greeted from behind the small check-in counter. "Is this one of your wedding guests?"

Katie nodded. "Sure is. I already checked her in, so I have her keys with me."

"We hope you enjoy your stay," the woman said to me before returning to her computer.

I followed Katie into the elevator and she pressed the

number *two* on the keypad. I leaned against the wall, yawning loudly and stretching my neck from side to side. "Ugh, I'm so tired. International jet lag is crazy."

"Well… I don't want to rush you since you just got off the plane, but Sean's mom—or *mum* as they call her, isn't that the cutest—wants everyone to meet up for dinner downstairs at eight for the welcome party. She's about as friendly as that math teacher we had in eighth grade, so maybe try to steer clear of her."

I groaned inwardly, noting I only had five hours to rest and acclimate to the time difference. But it was my job as Katie's best friend to put some concealer on the bags beneath my eyes and slap a smile on my face for the good of the wedding. I just hoped I could squeeze in a little nap before getting all gussied up.

Katie seemed to notice my unintentional frown as we stepped onto my floor and said, "I know you're probably really tired. If you want to not come down I seriously won't be mad."

"I'm not going to ditch my first chance to meet your future husband."

"Okay, so here's your key. I left one with the front desk in case you lose yours."

She pressed an actual key into my hand as she dropped my heavy bag to the floor with a thud. I looked down at the key. I couldn't remember the last time I went to a hotel and used an actual, metal key.

"Oh, I almost forgot, it's really just a cocktail thing, not like a sit-down dinner. You brought a couple of dresses right?"

"They might be a little wrinkled, but I'll have time to iron them."

"Thanks, love you! I'll see you tonight." She grinned and hopped back to the elevator, disappearing inside.

I let out a deep breath and opened the door to my room. It was quaint and clean with dark blue drapes and carpet that was offset by a wood four-poster bed with white, inviting bedding. As I dropped my suitcase heavily next to a small dressing table, I opened one of the windows that framed it and peered outside, letting a rush of cool, Scottish air stream in.

The sky was a bright and clear blue, making the white-wash of the buildings opposite seem to glow. The deep blue waters of the North Sea were beyond the roofs of several buildings. Below, there were cars and people milling the streets, but the old-world feel still sent a chill down my spine. I had never been out of the United States and Scotland seemed like an awesome place to start.

For the next ten days, I would be living it up with my best friend, drinking whisky with the locals, soaking in the history I craved, and attending what was promised to be a fairy-tale wedding. But first, I needed a fucking nap.

I HURRIED DOWN to the cocktail party only a few minutes late. I didn't think to set an alarm and slept a bit longer than I anticipated. By the time I naturally woke up, it was after seven, giving me less than an hour to make it look like I wasn't completely jet-lagged.

I managed a quick shower, leaving my hair piled on top of my head to keep it dry. Then I crossed to the wardrobe where my dress for the evening hung. It was one of my favorites, a deep purple, off-the-shoulder number that nipped in at the waist and had a high-low bottom. Seeing it was still a little wrinkled from traveling, I hung it up in the small bathroom and turned the shower on hot, hoping the steam would flatten out the fabric.

Small lamps on either side of the mirror lit the dressing table and I sat on the stuffed stool to do my makeup. I paired a smoky eye with my favorite deep red lip. My mom always said the burgundy shade made me look like a vampire due to my dark hair and pale skin, but she also still thought permed hair and frosted lipstick was the height of fashion, so I took her tips with a grain of salt.

By eight o'clock, I had rolled my sleep-mussed hair into voluminous curls and my dress was wrinkle-free. And by ten after eight, I had buckled the ankle straps on my open-toed pumps and shoved my room key, driver's license, passport, phone, and pounds into my matching black clutch. Only slightly late, but I assumed I wouldn't have been the only person to come in a few minutes after the official beginning.

I heard the party before I saw it. The sound of a gentle piano wafted through the lobby and down the hall and I followed it. The music led me to a nice-sized room where a dozen rectangle tables dotted the floor, draped in pristine white cloths. The low lighting and stone walls made it feel cozy and the small candles scattered about only added to the appeal.

I scanned the room for Katie. There were several faces I recognized—her parents, an aunt, some cousins, an uncle, and a grandfather—but most were strangers. I assumed that they were part of the groom's side, since by Katie's explanation the wedding as a whole would be an intimate affair, attended by only the nearest and dearest. And the fact that the majority of the strange men were wearing kilt.

"Rose, you made it!" Katie's mom Gloria engulfed me into a tight hug while her father, Steve, kissed me on the cheek. They had often acted in place of my parents while my own were too busy with their own shit to properly look after me. "We're all so happy you could come."

"Like I would miss it."

"How was your flight?"

"It was good. Is Katie here yet? I wanted to meet Sean."

She looked around, her lips pursed. "No, not yet. I think she said she wanted to make an entrance."

"Of course she did."

Katie was always one for drama. In our middle school's production of *Romeo and Juliet*, she had gotten the coveted role of Juliet. In the first performance, unbeknownst to our drama director, Katie had gone to the party store and gotten one of those knives filled with fake blood. So, on the night of the show instead of the clean, final stab that killed our fair maiden, Katie shrieked as she drove the dagger into her stomach again and again, staggering about the stage, dripping fake blood all over the front row of the audience. Needless to say, the drama director wasn't pleased, but since I was only 'woman number four' in the cast, it brightened my experience considerably.

A waitress came past me, carrying a tray filled with champagne flutes. I plucked one as she neared and sipped, the bubbles tickling my nose. Then I found a table to sit at where one of Katie's young cousins sat, playing with an iPad. My seat allowed me to survey the crowd as I waited for Katie and Sean's arrival.

Throughout college and the beginning years of my career to date, I had been the picture of dull respectability. I went to sleep early, stuck to a strict study schedule, and graduated with honors before stepping into an internship that later turned into a job. I had been in a sorority, but even those long nights out were kept strictly to Fridays and Saturdays. I had been the designated driver more than once and I never disappeared into the bedroom of a frat brother for a little fun.

My dating life post degree was no different. I'd meet a nice guy, we'd go to dinner and out for coffee, discussing monogamy before having missionary sex with the lights off. I didn't want to go into my thirties with nothing fun to remember. A no-strings-attached dalliance with a hot Scot seemed to be in order.

Loud applause jarred me from the hunt for plaid potential hookups. I rose from my chair just in time to see Katie make her entrance, Sean on her arm. I recognized him from the Facebook pictures she had shown me and I could agree with her that he was good-looking. He was made handsomer by the red-and-green kilt he wore, paired with a dinner jacket. But it was Katie who really glowed, and not just due to the flaming piles of curls upon her head that was topped with a shining, silver tiara. Her red-lipped smile was wide and showed her white teeth, which matched the lacy gown she wore.

I clapped along with everyone else as the couple strode through the crowd, shaking hands and kissing cheeks. I wanted to go right up and throw my arms around them— after officially meeting Sean of course—but politely waited my turn and let them pass by the rest of the guests before coming to me.

"Rosie!" Katie pulled me near. "Sean, this is my best friend Rose that I've told you *everything* about. Rose, this is my future *husband* Sean!"

"I'm so pleased to finally meet you," Sean said with a Scottish accent that was far lighter than I expected, clasping my hand tightly. "Kathryn's told me so much about your youth together, I almost feel as if I've known you for years."

"Same. I've been dying to meet you since... well, since Katie met you."

"Ah, a whole three months then?" he asked with a playful tilt to his voice.

"Just about that long. Getting last-minute tickets here wasn't easy."

I let out a low breath of relief when he laughed. When Katie had called me to gush about her whirlwind romance, I had been skeptical. She had always been a free spirit who threw herself fully into whatever she was doing and I hadn't been sure if she was making the right decision at first. But it looked like there was some sass behind the blue-blood surface and Sean might be able to keep up.

"Are your accommodations to your liking?" he asked. "I had hoped the castle would be ready in time for the guests, but when you have a shotgun wedding, I suppose you can't force already laid plans to go by your timeline."

"The room's great. I'm excited to see the castle though. Sounds really romantic."

He smiled a bit and glanced down at Katie. "Well, when your lass wants a castle wedding, you do the right thing and push up all renovations and prepare that horse and carriage."

"Sean's being dramatic," Katie cut in. "There's no horse and carriage."

"Only because you didn't ask for one," he pointed out. "And does that mean I should cancel the suit of armor I rented? I had just broken in the cod piece."

I stifled a laugh as Katie waved her hand in his face to shut him up before turning to me. "Anyway, we're hoping to make you fall in love with Scotland so you want to come at least twice a year."

Someone called Sean's name and he looked over his shoulder at the speaker before turning back to me. "Please excuse me, my father needs to speak with me."

The moment he stepped away, Katie was on me. "So? Do you love him? Isn't he the best? He's so handsome—"

"You guys look great together," I said honestly, squeezing her hand. "He seems really nice."

"I know, right? Now, can we get some drinks? Being a matrimonial goddess is making me thirsty and I need to get something before the welcome speech."

"You're giving a speech?"

She rolled her eyes as she pulled me to the bar. "Not my choice. It's only a little something."

When we had our glasses of champagne, Sean waved us over. He stood by a massive, unlit fireplace. The mantel was filled with little lit candles and vases of white roses, which were Katie's favorite. And as soon as Katie stepped by his side, the piano music stopped and all eyes were on them.

Sean slung an arm around Katie and waited patiently for the last few voices to drift off into silence. "Good evening," he began in a clear, even tone. "Kathryn and I would like to thank you all for joining us on such short notice. We know that our whirlwind romance made for whirlwind travel plans for all of you to get here in time. But when you meet someone you wish to spend the rest of your life with, waiting any longer than you need to seems impossible."

Then, as if on cue, Katie added, "As Sean said, we really appreciate you guys coming to celebrate our wedding, especially my family and friends from America. When I came to Scotland, I didn't imagine I would meet a man like Sean and never leave, and it means so much to me that you've come all the way here for us. We're not just joining our two lives, but our two families and we simply couldn't do it without you."

Sean lifted his glass in the air. "*Ceud mile failte*—a hundred, thousand welcomes!"

When we all took a sip and some young man dragged off Sean, Katie and I spent the next hour milling around together. We met some of the other guests and drank through the hotel's stock of French champagne. During our travels, I found that the majority of the men on Sean's side were married, much to my disappointment. Now, I wasn't on the prowl like some desperate divorcée hoping to make a point that I was still a bright, young thing, but when one was on a vacation and in such a romantic setting, it's hardly a stretch to want a little connection. I was beginning to think I wouldn't find one so easily, but then the heavens opened and *he* arrived.

"Rosie, have you met the best man?" Katie asked around

the straw tucked between her lips.

"I don't think so."

"Then I think it's time you met Lachlan."

I followed her gaze to the bar, my eyes settling on a tall, kilted shot of whisky. The man—apparently called Lachlan—turned at once to her call. His hair was dark blond, his shoulders broad, his trim waist swathed in the dark blues and greens of his ancestral people. He came to us. His eyes were a bright green, almost fake-looking, and framed with the kind of dark eyelashes that only men apparently had.

"Lachlan, this is my best friend and maid of honor, Rose," Katie introduced. "Rosie, this is the best man and Sean's cousin, Lachlan."

"Pleasure to meet ye, Rose." His accent was deeper and richer than Sean's.

It was like he was the full-bodied version of a Scotsman while Sean was the diet brand. It sent a delicious shiver down my spine.

"Good to meet you, too."

"I really want you guys to get along since we'll be doing lots of fun wedding stuff that you guys need to come to," Katie explained, leaning her head against my shoulder. "Rosie's my favorite girl person in the whole world and I want you to be nice to her, Lachlan."

I poked her crown away. One pointed tip was digging into my cheek. "I'm sure we'll have lots of fun," I assured her, vaguely wondering how many drinks she had, since I knew it had lapped my own number.

"Amazing," she gushed patting my shoulder and looking up at Lachlan, who appeared completely unfazed by her apparent drunkenness. "And you. You better look out for Sean when you guys go out for your stag night thing."

"Stag night?" I asked. "Like hunting?"

Lachlan laughed, a rich sound that brightened his already golden face significantly. "There is no' any huntin' involved. Well... no' that night in any case. It's a bachelor party in essence, just as ye have in America."

"I see. And does the bachelorette party have an equally fun name?"

"A hen night!" Katie explained. "It's going to be great. Sean's cousin Sorcha is going to take us to all these cool, local bars and we're going to get dressed up and I'm going to carry a pot of salt or something... I don't know, but it's going to be wild."

"No' too wild," Lachlan chastised good-naturedly then his eyes flitted to something beyond our heads. "Ach, there's the groom."

Katie perked up instantly and I had to detangle a lock of my hair from her crown as she spun to greet her fiancé. "Sean, you're still here!"

"Where else would I go?" He wrapped his arms around her. "Are you a bit heavy with drink then, Kathryn?"

"A *wee* bit," she admitted, her straw coming up empty in her ice-filled glass.

"I'll get you some water," I offered. I knew from experience that if Katie wasn't properly fed and hydrated after a night of alcohol, she would pay for it the next morning, as would anyone she came in contact with.

And what kind of maid of honor was I if I let my main girl get hung over on *my* first real day in Scotland? A shit one that was what I'd be.

I excused myself and went to the bar and asked the minder for a large glass of ice water and kept an eye out for one of the waiters that were bringing around the food.

When one finally passed me, I asked, "Hi, can I take all these mini burgers? They're for the bride." And confiscated the whole dish.

And once I got the water, I balanced the cup in the middle of several sliders and turned to go find Katie. But when I turned, I severely underestimated the delicateness of the whole operation and everything toppled over.

Now, if the mass of greasy meat, ketchup, tomatoes, onions, and lettuce had fallen to the floor and then splattered with a full glass of water, that would have meant a few apologies to the staff while I did my best to mop up my mess. Maybe even some nervous laughter on my part and a stain on my shoes. But the tray didn't go on the floor because the universe apparently hated me and didn't think I deserved nice things.

The whole tray went right into Lachlan's broad, muscular, handsome chest.

I stood there in horrified silence as Lachlan stared at me, his white dress shirt wet and smeared with condiments. I tried to say I was sorry—I tried to say anything—but the words got caught in my throat. But what did come out was a strained sort of rasping giggle. My greatest shame in life was that I had always been a nervous laugher. It didn't matter if it was Grandma's funeral or my own senior thesis dissertation on the effects of the fall of the Ottoman Empire on modern international trade deals in front of the faculty of my university, I would always be fighting peals of uncomfortable laughter brought on by my own nerves.

"Oh... I'm... I'm so sorry." I managed the horror that tightened my throat.

He raised a brow at me as a waitress passed him several white napkins and he whipped a great big glop of ketchup from the front of his kilt. It splattered on the floor beside his dress shoes. I was on the verge of mortified tears, feeling the eyes of the surrounding guests look over us in interest.

"Not a problem, it was only a family heirloom. Been so for two centuries, but no matter."

"Oh, no." I had dumped ten cheeseburgers and some ice water on a *family heirloom.* On my first night in Scotland, I had destroyed one of the many cultural icons that held a great deal of worth to many people. I was a monster in knock-off Jimmy Choos.

I grabbed a handful of cocktail napkins from the bar and dropped to my knees, attempting to busy myself with cleaning the floor, if only to avoid Lachlan's cool gaze. But as soon as I had placed the first messy burger back onto the tray, I saw a waitress was already there, picking up the pile and plopping it into a receptacle.

"No worries, miss," the waitress said soothingly, motioning for me to stand.

"No, please, let me—"

She smiled and gently took the glass shard I held. "I'll right it. It's standard procedure for broken glass."

"Thank you," I muttered, standing. "Lachlan, I'm really—"

"It's fine." His voice was soft enough, but I couldn't tell if he was just being polite for the sake of the party.

"I'll pay for the dry cleaning."

"Go deal with Katie, aye?" You would think it was a suggestion, but the tone made it clear that it wasn't up for discussion.

I nodded dumbly and stood, scurrying off to find my friend. I was happy that the bar was in an odd corner and few people had seen me destroy an irreplaceable plaid, but my cheeks still burned hot with leftover shame. It was just my luck that I would make such a terrible first impression on anyone in Scotland, especially one that was the metaphorical yin to my yang in Katie's wedding. I made a mental note to offer to pay for a new kilt altogether when it came to it.

I found Katie and Sean seated at one of the tables. She was sipping a glass of water, some sort of muffin dissected before her. She tipped her glass at me as I approached and Sean smiled pleasantly. It shamed me again to think that the family heirloom I had ruined was likely part of his family history as well.

"You got some water and something to eat. That's good." I tried to keep my tone even, but I thought the underlying humiliation might still be heard.

She nodded, taking a bite of her snack. "Yeah, Sean got them when you didn't come back right away."

"Oh, sorry about that."

"It's fine. Sean can take care of me."

Sean reached out and straightened her tiara. "I know the drill. Food, water, sleep... more food when she wakes up, just like a wee bear. Don't worry."

"Hey, it's getting pretty late and I'm a little jet-lagged. Is it okay if I duck out a bit early?" I asked Katie. "I'll be awake bright and early to start on my maid of honor duties."

"Totally! You were a trooper coming down for so long as it is."

I leaned down and hugged her. "Okay, I'll see you tomorrow then. Sean, it was really nice to finally meet you."

"Likewise," he replied warmly.

As I walked out of the event room and stepped into the elevator, I almost wished I had said something else to Lachlan instead of staring at him like an idiot and mumbling while he was coated in ketchup. He probably thought I was deranged and would hate me forever. I probably would if I were him.

My shame followed me up to my floor, into my room, sat on the bathroom counter with me as I washed the makeup off my face, and slid into bed beside me. It sat heavy and hot in the pit of my stomach and I couldn't relax enough to even dream of sleeping, something I really was looking forward to.

So instead of enjoying my first night in Scotland beside my best friend in the whole world, I had embarrassed myself and probably made an enemy for life.

Chapter Two

T HE MORNING LIGHT streamed into my hotel room window, filling the space with the kind of pure brightness one might expect to see in the Highlands. And for a moment, I basked in it, relishing the feeling of being cozy in bed and thinking about all the sightseeing I could do that day. I was going to go cake tasting with Katie in the afternoon, but I was a free girl until then. It didn't matter that I never liked cake, or maybe it was just the icing, but tasting was one of the jobs a good maid of honor took seriously.

I began mentally preparing my itinerary to fill my morning.

1. eat full Scottish breakfast—no blood pudding
2. find newspaper to take as souvenir
3. find gift shop for more souvenirs for myself and my mom
4. take a million pictures
5. buy as many history guides as I could manage to stuff in my bag

It was just enough to fill my morning without overexerting myself.

I leapt from bed and began stretching out my tired limbs, stiff from travel and sleep, noting it was seven in the morning. That was earlier than I thought, but I assumed my body was still adjusting to the time difference and that it would just promise me a solo breakfast.

Once I was dressed and had put enough makeup on to cover up the effects of international travel, I packed up my purse and left to go down to the small dining room to eat. It dawned on me that I might run into some of the people I had met the previous night and I wanted to be sure I knew their names if I did. There was Sean's cousin Sorcha, Sean's parents, some guy who was an uncle or maybe a neighbor, Lachlan—

My blood ran cold in my veins as the remembrance of what I had done washed over me like a freezing bath. I couldn't believe I had momentarily forgotten that I covered the poor man in cheeseburger and ruined his priceless kilt.

I could hardly choke down a cup of coffee and half a hot bun before leaving the hotel. No full Scottish breakfast for me. My usually voracious appetite had been squashed along with my pride, but I tried to brush off the feeling as I stepped into the warm Scottish, summer sun. Lachlan wasn't there, so it wasn't like I had to actually worry about him just yet.

The town was just as beautiful in the morning light as it

had been in the afternoon one, if just a bit quieter and warmer than before. There were still cars on the road and people on the sidewalk, but the businesses were just beginning to open. A woman propped her door open and began sweeping her stoop while another next to her flipped her *closed* sign to one that read *welcome*. It was a bakery and I made a mental note to stop there for breakfast one day.

I spent the morning milling around the town, really just going up and down several small blocks, checking out the small stores and picking up random trinkets and cute things that would fit in the second duffel bag I had prudently packed just for my purchases. As I lugged the bags of T-shirts and hand-painted prints, I hoped the duffel wouldn't fill up too quickly. But since I had already picked up three visitor guides and two books on Highland history on my first day, I wasn't too optimistic.

I also bought a bouquet of full, pink flowers on a whim, forcing me to also buy a vase to put them in. It was white, green leafy designs climbing up the sides. There was something intimate about going into the flower shop and being handed a freshly cut bouquet wrapped in brown paper and I inhaled their scent deeply as I went back to the hotel to meet Katie.

She was standing in the lobby when I came back down after dropping off my purchases and putting my flowers in fresh water. There was a thick binder under her arm, the papers and magazine clippings within emerging from their folders messily. I was surprised she'd thought ahead to such an item. Detailed planning was more my thing while she was normally one to just go with the flow and hope no one died.

"Hey, how are you feeling today?"

She rolled her eyes and heaved a heavy sigh. "Like shit. You?"

"Fine." I didn't feel like hashing out the disaster with the burgers just yet, not when I was going on my first maid of honor jaunt with the bride. "Is your mom meeting us at the bakery?"

"Nah. She gets herself too wound up about a lot of this stuff. She'd push for something totally old-fashioned and boring like vanilla on vanilla."

"Oh, the horror!" I said dramatically, watching as she stuffed a loose list back into its place.

"Yep. So I sent her off to this spa the next town over to make sure it's nice enough for some pre-wedding primping. I've actually already been there before and know that it's amazing, but she doesn't know that."

"You little sneak. It's smart though, giving your mom a dumb job to do."

"I'm just trying to survive. Anyways, we're just going down the street. I'm trying to keep things Scottish and really authentic for Sean's sake."

I followed her out of the hotel and we began walking down the same path I had first taken that morning. "Going traditional in that sense?"

"Completely. Local food, local entertainment, local dressmakers, all of it."

"Bagpipes?"

"*So* many bagpipes." She grinned and nodded to the other side of the road. "That's where our appointment is."

"Oh, I passed that place this morning."

A small sign sat over the door, *Sally's Sweets* embossed in black cursive. A bell tinkled as we entered and I was immediately assaulted with the sugary rich smells that accompany all forms of bakeries and candy shops. It made my mouth water and I could almost feel the cavities form as I scanned the glass case of delicate pastries.

A round woman in a pristine white apron came around the counter, her red cheeks raised in a smile. "Good day to ye both, I'm Sally. Ye must be Kathryn. Come on back, everyone's waitin' for ye."

"Who else is here?" I asked as we followed Sally though the bakery and down a short hall.

"Sean and Lachlan," Katie answered. "I told you that you guys would be spending a lot of time together."

The two men sat on one side of a worn, wooden table, a tray of colorful cake slices sitting untouched in the center. At each setting sat a plate, fork, and glass of water. I nodded to both politely, careful to not look directly at Lachlan, as Katie kissed her fiancé and took her seat beside me.

"Now, I've made up a bit o' each for ye to try," Sally began, motioning to the cakes. "There's a lemon sponge with a lemon buttercream. Next to that is a light vanilla with raspberry jam. And do ye see the darker one? That's the toffee. I also have the traditional vanilla, plain sponge, and red velvet. Ye'll see them all on the list there in case ye forget what's what."

"Wait, what's this one?" Katie asked, ignoring the list and pointing to the one closest to her.

Sally peered at it through her glasses. "That's the orange poppy seed. Very popular for summer weddings, as is this airy one with the rose petal jelly."

"Ooh, rose petal jelly," Katie whispered, elbowing me in her excitement.

"I'll leave ye to it," Sally said, turning to go. "Call me if ye need anythin'."

Katie immediately plunged her fork into the rose petal cake, moaning softly when she put the piece in her mouth. "Wow. This is the one, Sean."

Sean smiled warmly at her and then took a bite of his slice. "It's lovely, Kathryn, but don't you want to try the rest, just to be sure?"

"Oh, trust me, I'm going to try the rest. Seriously, Rosie, try this rose thing. It's like a garden is having a delicious orgy in your mouth."

"Aye." Lachlan caught my attention, his fork resting lightly on his bottom lip. "Do try it, Rose. It's only fittin', due to your name."

Katie giggled. "I didn't even put that together. See, Sean?

I told you this was the cake. It's good luck."

I tried to enjoy my bite with the other three watching me, but I could hardly taste it and it went down hard as I swallowed. It was difficult to relax when I sat directly across from Lachlan and I briefly wondered if he was testing me by poking fun at the rose petal cake. Either way, I needed to try and pull him aside afterwards to tell me how much to make the check out for. But until I could find a good moment, I plastered a smile on my face and nodded at every single thing Katie said.

But by the time Katie and Sean had narrowed down their choices to the lemon sponge, orange poppy seed, and the vanilla with rose petal, I felt sick to my stomach, and not all of it was due to the copious amounts of sugar. Lachlan's eyes were upon my every move, even though I kept mine focused on Katie and the cakes. He was studying me, taking me in, judging me for my clumsiness. I bet he was even waiting for me to flip the table over like a cast member on *The Real Housewives of New Jersey* and cover everyone with fondant like a pastry serial killer.

"Rosie, you in a sugar coma?" Katie was waving a hand before my face and I realized I had been staring at a slice of blueberry cake the entire time I had been giving myself the necessary pep talk.

"Oh, sorry. Still a bit jet-lagged," I covered smoothly, pushing my plate away. "So are you still at a standstill?"

Katie nodded, glaring at Sean. "Completely. I want the

rose stuff and he wants the orange, while we both think the lemon is pretty good, but not enough to really commit to."

"Why not do all three?" I asked, wondering what the issue was.

"All three?"

"Is that bad luck in Scotland or something to mix cake flavors? Because you could totally do a three-layer cake or even three separate cakes if you wanted to."

"I don't know." Katie leaned towards Sean. "Can we do a three layer? I mean, we only have about forty people coming."

Sean nodded, slapping the side of the head in that joking manner people have when they just discovered they were dumb. "Oh, aye. Of course we can, Kathryn. Why didn't we think of it? A three layer would be more than sufficient."

"Ugh, this is why you're my main maid," Katie cooed, leaning her head on my shoulder. "I've been in Scotland too long. My brain is like50 percent haggis and 50 percent kilt now or something. It seriously doesn't work anymore."

I stiffened at the mention of the word *kilt*, and tried to keep my expression straight. But my blood was traitorous and it pooled in my cheeks. It was all I could do to keep from glancing at Lachlan, who would probably be seething at the reminder of his dead heirloom.

"At least now you can check this off your wee list, Kathryn." Sean flipped open her bulging binder, turning right to the folder marked *cake* and making a small note in the margin. "All we need to do now is decide on the decoration. I'll leave that in your expert hands."

Katie pouted in the weird way she had when she was interacting with a man she liked and simpered, "Are you going to leave?"

"Aye. Lachlan and I are going to see to the special wedding surprise I have for you."

"Ooh, a surprise? What kind of surprise?" she asked as we both rose from our chairs to find the baker.

"Not telling." He smiled sweetly and stood, rounding the table and to kiss her softly on the lips.

They began whispering to each other, their faces barely touching. They were cute in a gross PDA way I would normally find offensive if it weren't my best friend. Seriously, it took them several minutes to stop their giggling and kissing. By the time they untangled themselves, I'm pretty sure Sean and Lachlan could have gone on their errand, come back into town, gotten a beer, and caught up on cricket, or whatever it was people watched in Scotland.

"Take care of my fiancée," Sean said as he took my shoulders and kissed me on the cheek. I had forgotten that was how some people said their goodbyes and awkwardly puckered at the air next to his face as he pulled away.

Lachlan was on deck, apparently finished kissing Katie. "Rose, nice to see ye."

As he began tilting his head downward, I panicked for some unknown reason. I overcompensated in a big way and lunged forward in order to get the whole weird cheek-kissing European thing over with ASAP. But spatial awareness has never been my strong suit and I—in turn—head butted him in the chin, fell against his chest, and let out a string of surprised profanities that would have made the Queen of England drop her teacup on a corgi.

"Oh, my God Rosie, are you okay?" Katie asked as I came to my senses.

It was then I realized I was basically cuddling with Lachlan. His arms were around my upper back and I was pressed against him like a swooning heroine on the cover of a cheesy romance novel. But instead of the dramatic zap of sexual tension between us, there was the corpse of a family heirloom we were just pretending didn't exist.

"Yeah, yeah." I pushed off with both palms against his chest, feeling a bit more chiseled muscle beneath them than I was really looking to find. "I just tripped over this chair." I motioned to the falsely accused offender as I backed away from Lachlan, my cheeks burning.

"Well, be careful. Can't have you in a cast in all the wedding pictures," Katie said, then snapped her binder back open and handed it to Sean. "Can you just take a look and make sure this photographer is the one you picked out? I need to call her today."

While Sean and Katie stood, heads bent over a page, I stared at Lachlan, trying to figure out a way to gently pull him aside. But I had a checkbook in my pocket and my big girl panties on, so I whispered, "Can I talk to you for a second, over there?"

He nodded and followed me over to the window. "What's up?"

I reached a hand into my bag and pulled out my wallet and a pen. "I seriously feel awful about what happened last night and—"

"Don't think o' it, Rose. It was an accident."

"An accident I'd like to pay for. Is a check okay? I can pay cash as well, but I'd have to find an ATM first."

"Really, Rose, it's nothin'." His voice was quiet and calm. I thought he was way too nice about the whole thing.

"Then let me pay for your… tux rental or something."

"You can pay me back by ignorin' it ever happened." He turned a looked at Sean, who tapped at his watch dramatically. "I'd best be off. We've an appointment to keep."

He and Sean took their leave and I went to stand beside the table, feeling a bit relieved but still guilty. "Jesus, I'm such a klutz."

"You literally never fall."

"Well… that's not totally true. I kinda dumped a plate full of sliders all over some family heirloom kilt of Lachlan's. Slammed right into him. It was like a BBQ murder scene."

She shrugged and began flipping through her binder until she reached a section full of pictures of elegant cakes. "So?"

"So I covered your future cousin-in-law in ketchup,

completely fucking up his kilt."

"Again… so? Just pay for dry-cleaning fees. Kilts are a dime a dozen here and it's not like his pattern is unheard of. I'm sure he probably even has a few."

I crossed my arms over my chest. "I tried just now. He told me it was some heirloom piece that was two hundred years old. He said it was totally ruined and still wouldn't let me pay."

Katie looked puzzled, her red brows knitted. "I didn't know they had any heirloom kilts."

"Yeah, well not anymore. I'm the heirloom killer."

"Is that why you were acting so weird?"

"Was it obvious?"

"You wouldn't even look at him and your eyes were all glazed over."

"You would be, too. I'm mortified."

"Was he mad?"

I nodded. Brushing my hair away from my face and trying to regain my composure. "I think so. It felt like he couldn't wait to get away from me."

She led the way into the main bakery. "He'll get over it. Lachlan isn't the kind to hold a grudge."

As I followed her around the bakery and looked over cake designs, I mulled over what she said, sincerely hoping she was right… for the good of the wedding.

Chapter Three

"**I** FEEL STUPID," Katie muttered under her breath as Sorcha handed her a brass pot, the light sound of sea salt rattling within.

We each had our own empty one, as well as a wooden spoon for beating it.

"It's tradition," Sorcha soothed. "Just bang it nice and loud at each pub."

I swiped another coat of dark purple lipstick on my mouth and straightened my matching light-up tiara. "Yeah, Katie Cat, loosen up."

She glared at me from under hot pink lids. "Also, does this color look good on me? I know redheads aren't supposed to wear pink. Since Savannah couldn't make it, I have all her green stuff and I could—"

"You wear pink all the time," I replied. "Sorcha's blonde, so she gets to be yellow and I look like death warmed over all the time, so I'm purple. Honestly, wearing tutus and tiaras out on the town is a lot more fun than the usual penis-themed event you'd get at home. I'm a fan of the dick-less crown."

Katie seemed satisfied with my answer and tucked her pot under her arm, preparing to leave the hotel in search of booze and coins. Sorcha had informed us it was tradition for us to go through the streets, into the pubs and bars, and bang on the pots like our lives depended on it. In response, the friendly townsfolk would drop cash into Katie's in return for a kiss. When I pointed out the whole "herpes is becoming an epidemic" thing, it was decided that a kiss on the cheek would do.

All decked out in our color coordinated tutus, our crowns flashing in their selected colors, we left the hotel. The night was slightly warmer than I expected for Scotland, making the trek to the first bar a lot more enjoyable than it could have been. We teetered down the street on our heels, Sorcha leading the way, banging her own pot. Katie and I tapped ours with a lot more reserve and we shared quick glances as we scurried behind.

"Here comes the bride!" Sorcha yelled as the first pub's doors swung open, only one block down from the hotel.

It was a small place with only around ten patrons, but they all raised their glasses as we entered and one man immediately held out a pound note. Katie's lips fell into a hard line, but Sorcha pushed her forward, a grin on her face. Sean's cousin was shaping up to be far wilder than him and it was going to be a pretty crazy night.

Katie let out a small shriek as the bearded man kissed her wetly on the cheek before dropping his money into the pot.

As soon as he left to go back to his friends, she said, "I need a fucking drink."

"Three shots of tequila!" I called to the bartender, digging out my money.

The gold liquid went down smooth and I was about to order another round when Sorcha shook her head. "No, only one drink at each bar."

"Only one drink?" Katie asked, straightening her *bride* sash. "How are we supposed to get drunk?"

"If we hit eleven bars and then start the round all over again, you'll be knackered in no time."

Sorcha began banging her pot again and led us out into the night to the next pub. It was admittedly much busier than the first, filled with people more our own age. There was a roar when we entered and guys began pulling out their wallets. Katie didn't look too pleased, but when the first ten-pound note landed in her pot and she took another shot of tequila, she noticeably relaxed.

"From the men down the end," the bartended said, pouring us each another shot.

"Does the one-shot rule still count if someone else if buying?" I asked, but Sorcha had already downed hers with a hefty wink at the group of guys who had sent the drinks our way. It was our first meeting, but I liked her.

Katie plucked hers off the bar and I followed suit. We clinked glasses before drinking. I wondered if we were allowed any other liquor besides tequila. It wasn't even a traditional Scottish drink... but maybe it was Scottish by association, since the bartender wore a kilt.

"What's the wee bride drinkin'?" A dark-haired man threw his arm over Sorcha's shoulders and she whipped around to face him.

"Danny Gordon?"

"The very same. Let me buy ye all a round!" he said, beckoning the bartended back our way with a wave of the hand. "What'll it be?"

I eyed the line of bottles behind the bar. "How about some whisky?"

His eyebrows rose. "Sorcha, ye've brought a bloody Yank to the pub!"

"Two." Katie smiled sweetly and rattled her pot. "If you wanna stay and chat, you gotta pay up."

Laughing, he dumped a handful of coins inside then ordered four shots before turning to us. When the glasses came, he toasted, "To the bride!"

"To the bride!" we all shouted.

I took a deep breath. The fine, Scottish whisky would have probably been amazing if it hadn't come after the tequila. But my stomach lurched and I leaned back against the cool wood of the bar, wondering how I was going to last through all eleven on Sorcha's list. It had been quite some time since I had partied all night and the last two bachelorette parties I had been to involved glasses of wine at a classy vineyard followed by dinner. Not a shot in sight.

"Okay, I need something greasy to combat all these shots," Katie said as she slapped her glass onto the table.

"Already?" Sorcha frowned, as if lamenting how American we were. "Then let's go get a bite at one of the finer establishments in Nairn."

"Room for one more?" Danny sounded hopeful, but Sorcha shook her head.

"Sorry, Danny, lasses only. It's a hen night after all."

"Who was he?" I asked as we stepped out onto the sidewalk.

Sorcha waved a hand dismissively. "Just Danny. Our families go way back, like to the clan days."

"He's cute."

"Aye, and I remember when it was five and pissed in my mum's rose bushes. Nice lad though."

"Where are we going?" Katie asked.

"I told you, one of the finest establishments for late night feasts of the drunken variety."

We followed Sorcha down the dimly lit streets, our heels clacking noisily on the stone as we went. She steered us to a small shop that was tucked between two closed stores. The single, wide window lit the sidewalk and I could smell the fry oil as the door swung open, beckoning us in.

"Fish and chips?" I peered around the little eatery, empty save for two teenagers behind the counter. They didn't seem at all interested in our festive, flashing garb, so hen parties were probably a common sight.

"The finest eatery in all of Nairn," she confirmed before placing all our orders.

I went with Katie to sit down at one of the small tables and we stowed our pots beneath our seats. She glanced down inside hers. "I'm making minimum wage tonight."

"Is that good or are you offended?"

"I'm not sure. I'm feeling the tequila, though."

"Me too," I confessed, my eyesight suddenly going a little lopsided. I giggled, taking in Katie's hot pink ensemble again. "Sorcha's handling it like a champ. I thought all our years in a sorority would have prepared us for this, but maybe we're just old?"

Katie scowled. "Never."

"Fresh from the sea." Sorcha dropped a tray with three sodas, a pile of fried fish, and thick cut fries on the table before falling into her own seat. "Let's eat fast, though. We have a tight schedule of debauchery to meet."

I felt pretty weird in that moment, eating fish and chips in Scotland, wearing purple from head to toe. But it did bring me back to my youth, to the rare nights of themed frat parties and staying out with my sisters, eating fried foods without worrying about bikini season. And after all, I did go all the way there to step away from my straight-laced work as a paralegal and all the endless boredom of paperwork, pantsuits, and meetings to discuss dividing up marital assets that was my everyday life.

Oh, God. I finally admitted it in my semi-drunk state.

My life *was* boring and sitting in a tutu at eleven at night in another country was the most exciting thing that had happened to me in years. I had spent most of my time after graduating working at my career, going to meetings, clawing my way up the ladder, and being so *boring*.

"We need to go drink. *Now*," I announced loudly as soon as we finished our food.

Sorcha looked pleased and she rose at once. "That's the kind of attitude I like to see!"

The next bar was much like before. We went in, banging our pots, me with more gusto than before. One shot each and a round of kisses to Katie and we were off to the next spot. But the tequila and whisky had joined forces against us and they were taking no prisoners.

"Please, no more shots," Katie moaned. "Weak cocktails only."

"Don't worry yourself, we'll stay at the next one a bit. Do either of you like to dance?" Sorcha asked, a mischievous glint in her eyes.

The pub was more of a nightclub, tucked in between two darkened stone buildings. But I could feel the music before we even went in the doors. The rhythmic beats vibrated into the road and excitement built in my chest, something that was heightened by the liquor.

The boisterous crowd beneath the strobe lights barely noticed our arrival. It was a stark contrast to the other, smaller pubs, and I was glad to see it. Katie began shoving her kissing cash into her clutch and Sorcha collected the pots and wooden spoons. She obviously recognized the girl behind the long bar because the bartender tucked them neatly out of sight, leaving our hands and arms free for the first time all night.

"What do you want to drink?" I yelled in Katie's ear. But then I saw that the bartender was already opening up a tab under Sorcha's name.

"I guess we don't have much of a choice."

I applied another coat of lipstick as we walked over to Sorcha, who slid a mojito to each of us. Again, I thought it was weird that I would be in a small town in Scotland and still be drinking the same drink as I would back in Jersey. But I could never turn down a good mojito.

The cold, sweet mix rejuvenated me and I found my mouth splitting into a smile as the three of us went onto the crowded dance floor. It was crazy how no matter where in the world I was, club music was all the same—the thick beat reverberating in my chest. But my dance moves didn't improve with the change of location. However, Katie was never a great one either, so we could just be uncoordinated together.

"Kathryn!" a voice called from somewhere in the crowd.

Katie's eyes were closed as she danced, the mojito's straw tucked between her lips. Sorcha had already found a man to partner up with and hadn't heard Katie's name either. I thought I heard a call again, but ignored it, focusing on my hips and the delicious mint concoction I wanted another of.

Katie's sudden stillness jarred me out of my disjointed moves. When I followed her gaze, I saw only her fiancé. Clad in a garish costume that looked straight out of *Braveheart*, Sean stood behind Katie, his face streaked with blue paint. There were several men behind him, similarly dressed in billowing white shirts and dark plaids and I stared at them for a moment in wide-eyed interest, wondering if I was hallucinating. Then I realized they were all dressed up for the stag night.

I burst out in laughter. Seeing them all there, decked out like some escapees from a renaissance fair, lit up by multicolored stage lights and fog, was unreal... and not just because *Braveheart* was terribly historically inaccurate. If one could ignore that, then it was just so fitting to see obnoxious-looking Highlanders, even if the location was terribly wrong.

I wiped away a few stray tears, thankful for waterproof mascara and tested that my purple fake lashes were still intact. Unfortunately, my cup was empty. So I left Sorcha, who was entangled in her stranger's arms, and Katie, who was sucking face with her future husband, and made my way shakily to the bar. The music, drinks, and alcohol were washing over me like a fuzzy wave of mint and lime.

To keep myself upright while I waited for the busy bartender, I leaned my elbows on the top of the bar. I wanted a fresh drink and a dance... with a hot guy. There was no shortage of men in the club, and I was sure I could find a more than willing partner. All I needed to do was find a guy who fit my physical criteria of a worthy man—tall, strong shoulders, chiseled jaw, the whole nine yards. A kilt would be a plus.

"Yes, a kilt," I said to myself. "I need a kilt."

"At your service," a deep voice at my side said.

I turned around, seeing a man looming over me. His face was streaked with blue and he was shirtless under the plaid of his kilt. I laughed, wondering which of the single friends and cousins he was. Katie had told me only the unattached guys were going out on the town.

"Fancy a drink, do ye?"

I nodded, taking in the smooth muscle of his bare chest and shoulder. A tattoo sat on one pectoral. It looked like some kind of reindeer or maybe a moose head. I leaned in and squinted in the dim light, trying to get a better look, but it was like the animal was wiggling around and I couldn't focus.

The man laughed. "Drunk?"

"Drink," I said, straightening up and pushing my empty glass into the waving hand of the man with said tattoo. "A mojito."

"Bossy lass." His words were stern, but his eyes glazed over me in an appreciative way that made me smile. It had been quite some time since a man had looked at me with such unmasked lust and I reveled in it.

He leaned over the bar, catching the attention of the bartender almost instantly. I watched him as he talked. I thought I should know him, but my eyes couldn't quite decide and my mind was fuzzy and all I wanted to do was dance—to forget about everything like when I was in college and Katie and I would hit bars and clubs, never paying for a drink, and always coming home at the end of the night with new phone numbers in our cells that I almost never called.

A cold glass was put into my hands. I closed my eyes and drank heavily, hardly tasting the alcohol. "This is weak."

The man—whom in my head I nicknamed *Braveheart*—took the cup from me and took a sip. "No, it's made well. Maybe you're a bit more drunk than ye think."

"Listen, William Wallace, while you were off fighting the English and getting revenge for your murdered wife, I was drinking mojitos at the Delta Delta Kappa fraternity house. Trust me. This drink is shit and spits on the graves of its ancestors."

"Then I'll take it back."

"Come on, Braveheart. Let's dance."

I dragged him onto the floor, catching Katie's eye as Braveheart settled himself behind me, his hands on my hips. She smiled and I returned the gesture, leaning back towards my partner. His fingers ran the length of my waist as we swayed to the music. His breath was in my ear and I savored the feeling of the sturdy form behind me. It had been so long since I had a man's arms around me and I could have melted into his embrace.

But wasn't that exactly what I wanted? To melt into a man's embrace? To sow my wild oats in Scotland with a kilted man? Braveheart was as good a man as any and if his upper body was any indication of what hid beneath the folds of his plaid, I was in for a good time.

Several songs had come and gone by the time I struck up the nerve to invite Braveheart back to my hotel room. The tequila only offered so much liquid courage and I needed one more shot to pry the words from my lips. And apparently that one shot was all I needed because as soon as we both put down our glasses, I found the strength.

I reached up, putting my hand on Braveheart's shoulder and pulling him down. "Wanna come back to room?"

"I thought ye'd never ask."

With a wave to Katie and Sorcha, Braveheart and I scurried from the club. I was grateful for how strong he was, as I was having a hard time staying upright in my sky-high heels. We barely made it out the door before he pressed me against the cold, stone wall. His mouth fell upon mine, his hand skimming my hips, my bare arms, my neck. When he pulled away, I was panting with need for more.

"I'm at *The Wild Thistle*. Do you know where that is?"

"It's merely down the road."

I tasted the liquor on his tongue when we kissed; he was also pretty drunk. But he held himself well and made sure I didn't fall on my face, which was always a major plus when it came to getting in my pants. His hands were firm and strong and I couldn't wait to see what else they could do.

"Good evening, ma'am," I said to the front desk woman in my best *no-I-am-not-drunk* voice as we passed.

As soon as we were in the elevator though, I burst into laughter, which Braveheart quickly silenced with his lips. If I was more intoxicated, I might have let him lift my dress up right there, but I managed to press my floor number and even dug my room key out of my clutch without ever breaking the kiss.

We fumbled down the hall in a bustle of roaming hands and mouths, practically falling into my room as soon as I unlocked the door. He barred it shut, moving away from me for just a second, them coming to me again. He tossed me onto the bed and unbuckled both my pumps, throwing them onto the floor. His boots followed and he crawled on top of me, cupping my breast in one hand while his lips explored the curve of my neck and collarbone.

I ran my fingers through his blond hair as I yanked my light-up, purple tiara and lost it somewhere on the bed. It offered the only light in the room, save from the one from a streetlamp that crept in through the sliver between the partially shut curtains. But I liked the darkness. It added a certain level of mystery and danger to our drunken rendez-vous, which in reality wasn't so dangerous since he was related to Sean.

When I dared to lift the edge of his kilt, I frowned, feeling terribly betrayed. "You're wearing *shorts*?!"

He laughed and unwound the rest of the plaid, leaving him in a pair of gym shorts, complete with pockets. "Where else was I going to put my wallet and keys?"

"A sporran like a normal Scotsman?"

"I keep my sporran for special occasions." He nipped at my shoulder. "Forgive me?"

I wanted to be angry with him, but I had to admit I understood his need for a safe place for his stuff without wanting to ruin a nice bag in a bar. I never took my best purses with me when I went out to bars. But I wouldn't let him know how easily my forgiveness came.

"What are you going to do to make me forgive you for such treachery?"

He didn't answer, but ripped off my purple tutu, leaving me in the tank top I wore with it, along with my underwear. He fingered the delicate white lace between my thighs and I wished he would tear them off me as well. I was too needy, too turned on to wait for him to warm me up. I was as ready to go as I would ever be.

I reached down and pulled my top off over my head then unhooked my bra with one hand, throwing it aside. His green eyes grazed my body hungrily and he let out a faint growl of approval when I began sliding my panties down my hips.

"Hurry the fuck up, Braveheart."

His eyes flashed and he took out his wallet, pulling out a condom. He tore the wrapper open with his teeth as he kicked off his shorts. I was pleased to see that his lower body matched the perfect upper without fault. I barely saw him roll on the condom in the darkness before he was inside me, filling me with one swift movement.

I arched my back as he began to move, his back muscles rippling beneath my palms. His fingers kneaded my breasts and his mouth covered mine. I couldn't believe I had waited so long to have sex again and thought Braveheart was the perfect man for the job of getting me back in bed, even though his kilt was only a costume.

Historically, my dates had been stale and boring. And when I did decide to attempt a relationship, it ended up being the kind that always ended up fizzling into nothing. I had craved some real passion, the kind that curled my toes and made my stomach twist with longing. Now I had it between my thighs and I never wanted to give the feeling up.

He lifted my leg, allowing him greater access, and I cried out, my nails digging into his arm as he hit some new, deep spot within me. The build up of an orgasm began to swell and by his quickening pace he felt the same. As the final sharp spike of desire hit, I wanted to call out his name, but it dawned on me I had no idea what it was, and I certainly didn't want to be yelling out "William Wallace!" and have him reply with "Freedom!" like Mel Gibson... well, at least I didn't think so.

I bit my lip to stop the wave of laughter that hit me square in the middle and tried to focus instead on his body above mine and the intense pleasure it just brought me. We were only going to be together for one night. Names didn't matter.

Chapter Four

I WOKE UP in a tequila-tinted haze. My head felt thick and the slim strip of sunlight that came in through the window was blinding. It took me a moment to remember the night before, but when I did, I was pleased to know it had been a wild one. And when I tried to slowly sit up, something stopped me. It was an arm, a sleeping man's arm. His face was buried in a pillow and all that was visible were his scratched-up shoulders and a shock of dark blond hair.

Wracking my pounding brain for a name, all I came up with was Braveheart. That wasn't real, but I couldn't recall why that was the only thing that came to mind. But I couldn't stop and ask too much. I needed to pee. Fast.

I slid out from beneath his arm and wrapped myself in the floral maid of honor robe that had been in my room when I checked in. The tile floor in the bathroom was cold on the bottom of my feet and I peed hurriedly, wanting to get back into the warm, dark cocoon of the bed, regardless of my guest.

When I went to the sink to wash my hands, I caught sight of myself in the mirror and gasped. Purple and blue marked my face and neck, but it wasn't bruising, it was paint and makeup. I had forgotten the men had been dressed like Braveheart, complete with the historically inaccurate face paint.

I hurriedly scrubbed my face and neck clean, but then caught sight of my body in the open robe. There were blue smears on my breasts, thighs, and stomach. It left a clear map off all the places the man's mouth had been. And it looked as if it traveled all around the globe. I wiped at them hurriedly, knowing I would need to shower as soon as my sleepover buddy gathered his shit and left. While I loved a good romp as much as the next single girl, I wasn't looking to be permanently marked.

He was still motionless as I crept back into the bedroom and for a moment I wondered if he was dead. I hadn't exactly been quiet in the bathroom and he still hadn't moved. I thought about waking him up, but I also wanted to know his name. He had probably told me at some point in the club, but I couldn't remember it for the life of me.

Then I saw it, my saving grace. His wallet sat on the nightstand.

I tiptoed to it and eased the leather open. I flipped through the bank notes and into the little slits where the cards were kept until I found his license. Tilting the pink card towards the sunlight, I read the name next to the picture of the man I knew all too well. My stomach dropped and my blood ran icy in my veins.

Lachlan James Calder Mackinnon.

"No," I whispered to no one in particular.

I couldn't figure out how I didn't recognize him. It wasn't like he was wearing a full coverage Halloween mask. He had on some face paint—that was it. I wondered if that was how Lois Lane felt with Superman throwing a pair of glasses on and instantly becoming Clark Kent. I always laughed at how dumb she must have been, but now I was no better.

And I wasn't wearing any kind of wild costume either. It was basically just a little dress and some purple accessories. Had he recognized me? Did he know who he was kissing up against the side of the club? Or had he also been as drunk as I had been and didn't realize who had taken him up to their room? I had gone out looking for some fun and brought home the best man!

I had tucked the license back into the wallet, returned it, and was just questioning if I should pack all my stuff up while he was sleeping and beg the front desk for an emergency room change when there was a sharp rapping on my door.

My head whipped to the bed, but Lachlan hadn't moved. I scurried to it, opening it a sliver to find Katie beaming up at me, looking fresh faced and well rested.

"Morning! Want to do brunch? They have the best menu and I'm starving and—"

Lachlan must have woken up when Katie knocked. I heard the light creaking from the bed as he moved. His eyes closed, and fully nude, he stumbled into the bathroom, not noticing the two women who were gaping at him from the door.

"Oh… my… God."

I grimaced and turned back to Katie. "Look, I—"

"I knew there was a spark there. I knew it!"

"No, it's not like that!"

Her eyes travelled from my mussed hair to my bare shoulders, which were still streaked with faint hints of blue. "Suuure, whatever you say."

"Seriously, Katie, I—"

The bathroom door opened and Lachlan passed, looking at us through one eye in the bright light through the hall. His face was clean of blue and purple, although I saw a smear of my lipstick on his chest. He stopped and yawned and said, "Mornin' Kathryn… Rose." He turned to go back towards the bed and I could tell the exact moment when he realized he was there in the nude. His broad shoulders tensed and his hands went to his front to cover himself, although all we could see was his backside, which was too good to be covered up.

"I'll meet you downstairs," I hissed, shutting the door in her face.

I took several deep, sobering breaths before turning to face Lachlan. He looked just as surprised to see me, and I wasn't sure what to make of it. We obviously had a good time, and if he was game, I thought maybe we could do it again, have a little more pre-wedding fun. I wasn't sure if I had what it took to keep things fun and drama-free, but I thought I could. I could have my passionate fling and return to my life, no harm, no foul.

"Hello," I said as I entered the bedroom area.

"Hello," he replied, not looking at me, as he pulled on his boots.

Not knowing what to do, I began tidying up my things, picking up my discarded bra and tutu, shoving them into my suitcase and out of sight. There was no telling where my panties ended up, but I figured I could search for them once Lachlan left.

When he had put on his boots and his kilt was folded up and tucked beneath his arm, he stood, running his hand through his hair. I had to admit the motion really highlighted the trim muscles of his torso.

"Well... I should be off," he said, rising to his feet.

For some reason it stung. He didn't ask to go to breakfast or to see if we could see each other again in a non-wedding aspect. He seemed really into me the night before and his obvious brush-off caught me off guard.

"Me, too. Katie's waiting for me."

His eyes darted around the room, looking everywhere but at me. It was almost insulting, since I was dressed only in a thin robe, but I brushed it off. "I suppose I'll be seein' ye at the next... wedding... thing."

"Yep."

I waited for him to say something else or maybe give me the customary kiss on the cheek, but it didn't come. He just looked at me like I had something weird on my forehead and nodded. He left my room, leaving me standing there, blue paint on my body and egg on my face.

"YOU'RE FINALLY HERE!"

If I said Katie looked pleased to see me, it was an understatement. She was practically bursting with joy as I sat down at the small table in the hotel's breakfast room. I had come down after a quick shower and some clean clothes that covered up the smears of blue that apparently didn't want to wash off very easily. The water also helped to clean me of my embarrassment that Lachlan obviously didn't want to see me again. Aside from an older couple that was some distant relation of Sean's I had met the other night, we were alone.

"Chill out, Katie." I picked up the brunch menu and skimmed the choices. My body craved food, but my stomach was in turmoil.

"How can I when I just found you in bed with my future cousin?"

"By chilling out."

A waiter appeared to take our orders and I got French toast, black coffee, bacon, and eggs. Katie ordered the same, probably more to get back to the conversation than because she craved simple carbs and fried meat. Besides, she hardly ever drank coffee at home, surviving on her natural energy levels that seemed to be never ending.

"So… are you ready to tell me what's going on?"

"There's nothing going on," I said as coffee was poured before us. I added cream and sugar until it was the perfect shade of light brown. "Honestly, I didn't even know it was Lachlan I went home with last night."

Katie rolled her eyes, her spoon clinking in her cup as she stirred her coffee. "How? It's not like you don't know him."

"I don't know. I was a little drunk and he had that face paint on and it was dark. We just had this really good chemistry and we went with it."

She raised her brow, still looking rather unconvinced. "And you seriously didn't recognize him?"

"I really didn't know it was him until I went through his wallet and looked at his license." I sipped my steaming coffee, hoping the cup hid my flaming cheeks that I was sure were red.

"You little hussy," she hissed. "You were so wasted you didn't even know it was Lachlan!"

"I know. I'm really embarrassed that it was him, of all people."

"Why? He's a good-looking guy, you're both single… he lives in the same country as me so we can basically be neighbors when you marry him…" Her tone was casual, but she was going to miss living in New Jersey with me. The distance would be hard on both of us.

"Neither of us meant to sleep together. It just kinda… happened. Trust me, he was just as surprised this morning."

"What, did he trip over his kilt and land in you last night?"

I shot her a dirty look, keeping my lips sealed while the waiter dropped off our food. I cut into my French toast with a little more force than necessary and said, "That's hilarious and everything, but Lachlan and I are both very embarrassed about the whole situation and we are never going to speak of it again."

"Oh, did he say that?"

"No… not exactly."

"Then what *did* he say?"

"He said nothing."

Katie stared at me in the weird way she always did when she thought I was bullshitting her. One brow went up and her mouth twisted up. "Seriously Rosie, he didn't say anything?"

"No. He looked at me really strangely and… left."

"That's it?"

"Yeah. I thought we had a really good time, but maybe I'm not cut out for one-night stands. The morning after really didn't feel as good as I thought it would." I shrank a little in my seat. Saying my thoughts out loud was making them real and I wasn't a fan. "Seriously, Katie, you should have seen the way he was looking at me. It was like I grew a horn."

"No way, he's probably just hungover."

"We just got off to a weird start and now we've made it even weirder and I just want you to have a good wedding," I finished lamely, watching as she polished off the last of her bacon.

"And I'll have a good wedding if you just relax and have a good time. Sleep with Lachlan, marry Lachlan, never speak to Lachlan again… I don't care. I just want to enjoy the next week with you before I'm off being an old married lady and you're back in the US."

"Ugh, what am I going to do without you?"

"Screw a lot less Scottish men… but that just sounds like it would be a pity."

Not wanting to dwell too much on the future, I decided to bring the conversation back to wedding planning. "So what's the deal with the bridesmaid dresses?"

Her eyes went wide. "Oh my God, with all the parties and everything, I haven't even thought to take you to go look at your dress! Sorcha's been, but of course she lives here, but I totally forgot about you."

"That's okay. Let me know the name of the store and I'll set up my own appointment."

"No need. We can just go there after we're done if you're not too tired. It's a small shop so I don't think it'll be a problem if we just drop by."

We finished our brunch, staying on the safe conversation

of flowers, table linens, and made plans to go see the venue the following day. For a little bit, it felt like old times, when we both were in college and then later when our offices were only a few blocks away and we would meet for drinks after work and then go shopping. God, I was going to miss my best friend.

THE DRESS SHOP was very much like the bakery where Katie had gotten her cake. Tucked between a tack shop and a row of stone-fronted homes sat a small store with a front that showed off a line of frilly kids' dresses and equally frilly adult counterparts. I immediately feared the gown I would be forced into would be some hot pink monstrosity. But, I was maid of honor. I could wear any hideous outfit with pride.

"Good afternoon, dears." A thin woman came from around a mannequin as soon as we entered. "Kathryn, hello!"

"Hi, Sylvie. This is my maid of honor, Rose. I'm really sorry for the short notice, but I was hoping that if you weren't too busy, she could try on her dress?"

"O' course! Ye sent me all her measurements already, so as long as she has her shoes, I can make sure it fits well." She turned and beckoned us to follow.

As we trailed her back to the fitting rooms, I was pleased to see the majority of the dresses inside were perfectly normal and not covered in bows the size of my head. All said, I wasn't sure exactly what the dresses looked like, only that they were a pale blue—almost gray—to compliment the men's kilts.

I left my purse with Katie beside the triple full-length mirror after getting my shoes from inside. We had gone up to my room before leaving for the shop and I hoped, for the sake of Sylvie, the dress would fit. If it didn't, then I would probably be in a bit of trouble. There probably wouldn't be enough time to get too many alterations done.

Sylvie helped me into a simple, strapless dress. The light fabric crossed over the breasts and hugged me lightly round the waist. The skirt flowed down and around to the tips of my toes like a waterfall. They usually tell people when they buy some ugly bridesmaid gown, "oh, shorten it up and wear it again!" to try and make them feel better about spending three hundred dollars on some yellow crime against humanity they'll shove into the back of their closet... but I loved the dress.

When I stepped out of the fitting room to go to the mirrors, Katie let out a loud sigh. "Rosie... you look amazing."

"Because this dress is amazing."

"Ooh! Wait, stick your right leg out, there's a surprise!"

Confused, I stretched out my foot, revealing a slit that ran up to my thigh. "Wow, didn't see that coming."

"Secretly sexy!"

"It's so pretty. Really, Katie Cat. I'm so grateful you didn't pick something terrible."

"I couldn't do that. I'm going to have to look at the wedding pictures for the rest of my life. I don't want you to look hideous, that would only punish myself."

"How's the fit?" I asked Sylvia, who was inspecting the hem.

"Quite nice," she replied, rising to her feet to look at the hidden zipper. "I do no' think ye need any alterations. How do ye feel?"

"Awesome. This dress is beautiful."

Sylvia smiled warmly and then helped me to unzip the back a little so I could get changed back into my clothes. Once I was dressed, she took the gown into the back of the shop to put it into a garment bag for me.

"Should we take it back to the hotel?" I asked as I handed Sylvia my card.

Katie shook her head and toyed with a display of floral hairclips. "No, don't worry about it. Sylvia is going to have all the dresses delivered to the venue the morning of."

"Aye, that's right. Just leave it with me and I'll see it gets where it needs to go," Sylvia said as she passed me my credit card and receipt.

I thanked her, and Katie and I stepped out to the warm, early afternoon light. The day had cooled slightly and I hoped it would rise again in time for the wedding. Katie had told me we would be outside for the ceremony and that the venue had wonderful gardens. It would be a shame if we had to move everything inside due to weather. It wasn't cold enough to warrant a coat, but I shivered in my T-shirt and jeans.

"What next?" I asked as I pulled on my cat-eye sunglasses.

"Hmm... what haven't you seen in Nairn?"

"Everything, besides the inside of some bars."

"Then come on, we should go to the waterfront."

Katie led me down the main road, although calling it a main road might have been a bit dramatic. It wasn't the bustling highway like the one I drove down every day for work back at home, but it was a wider street with a bit more traffic on it than I had seen in other places in Nairn. As we passed the small groups of people congregated outside ice cream parlors and trinket shops, I heard various languages and accents. The closer we got to the ocean, the more the town evolved into a tourist locale.

I smelled salt in the air as the end of the road came into view, letting on to a wide expanse of sandy beach, which stretched out into the blue-grey waves of the sea. It wasn't warm enough to lie out and tan or go for a swim, but the sun beat down, keeping the chill away. There were also small fishing boats and sailboats scattered in the water. It reminded me of how Sorcha had called the small fish and chips shop the finest establishment in the city and I knew she was right now, seeing that those same boats probably brought in the fish.

We took a left and strolled down the sidewalk, the beach

on one side and rows of small shops on the other. Unlike the area near my hotel, these had their goods spilling out into the open, tempting people in with shirts, glassware, seashells, and stones. When I spied a large store with a bright, plaid painted door, I dragged Katie inside.

"Rosie, this place is for tourists," she hissed as the bell above us jangled loudly.

I pushed my sunglasses on top of my head. "And *I'm* a tourist."

She didn't answer me, but followed me around the shop as I looked at all the souvenirs and trinkets. I settled on several magnets with pictures of castles and Scottie dogs on them, a calendar featuring photos of flower-covered hills, and old ruins for the next year, a hat with the Scottish flag for my dad, and a mug lined with small thistles. Touristy? Yes, but who knew when I would have the chance to be a tourist again?

"Hungry?" Katie asked as we stepped back out to the sidewalk. Girl had a bottomless pit for a stomach. "I'm craving something sweet."

We went a few blocks down to a small ice cream shop. It was the old-fashioned kind where the homemade goods came in only a handful of flavors that were changed daily to suit the season and the local tastes. Even the cones looked handmade, perfectly formed and covered in sugar.

We each got two scoops of chocolate and caramel sea salt in waffle cones and I had just taken the first lick when Katie asked, "Want to see something cool?"

I nodded and she led me to the back of the shop, past some small, round tables that were mostly occupied by other patrons. We went to a narrow, metal, spiral staircase that led upwards to the second floor. I wasn't sure what to expect, but as Katie had obviously been there before, I trusted her judgment.

The second floor opened up to a large, open, rooftop patio filled with tables that were topped with colorful umbrellas. We sat beside the low railing overlooking the water and ate our ice cream. For a moment, it almost felt like we were back in New Jersey. We spent many summer nights on the boardwalk in small places just like that one.

"This is really making me miss Savannah," I said. "Remember the time your parents were away for a week and we all came home to stay at your place over break? We were on the Ocean City boardwalk almost every night eating popcorn and funnel cake."

"We should call her."

"Now?"

"It's morning there and it's not like she'd answer if she was elbow deep in some lady." She reached into her purse and pulled out her cellphone. She scooted her chair beside me and pressed the FaceTime button.

Savannah's smiling face almost immediately came into view. Her caramel colored hair was tied in a bun atop her head and I recognized her living room wallpaper behind her.

"Hey, you guys!"

"Savannah, we miss you," Katie said. "We've been so wrapped up in wedding things, we just wanted to say hi."

"Sunshine and ice cream? I'm so jealous. I attended a birth last night and I only just got home. I'm waiting for my Chinese food to come and then I'm going to bed."

"We need to get together when I come home," I said. "I'll come visit for a weekend or something, whenever you're not too busy assisting in the miracle of life."

She rolled her eyes. "You guys are so dramatic. Oh, there's the door. I gotta go. Love you guys!"

We both said goodbye and the call ended. I really did miss her. After college, she moved to Pennsylvania to be near her parents and start on her midwifery career. There was only a six-hour drive between us, but after a long week at the office, the distance seemed too great. But it was less than a plane ride, so I was running out of excuses.

"So…" Katie began, her voice a little too casual. "You and Lachlan might want to… you know… hang out again?"

I rolled my eyes. "I thought we moved past this."

"Nope. No moving."

"We'll only be hanging out only for strict wedding purposes."

"Mm-hm."

"I'm serious. It was a one-night thing because we were both drunk and made a mistake. The look on his face made it clear he wasn't too pleased."

She took a large bite of her cone, studying me. "Would it be so bad if it happened again? I mean, not to be all incest-y, but he's a good-looking guy."

"It's not incest if it's your husband's cousin."

"Still. I'm just saying that he's good-looking, you're good-looking, it was probably just a big misunderstanding."

I ignored her and focused on my ice cream, which was suddenly not as delicious as it was a few minutes before. Instead, my mind wandered to Lachlan. Katie was right that he was a good-looking man, muscular in all the right places with a jawline that was so sharp, it could cut glass. Everything about him screamed sex, but what was supposed to be a night of fun was far less satisfying in the morning. I wasn't disappointed that I had woken up beside Lachlan, but it seemed like he might have said the opposite.

"Yeah, he's hot, but it was one night. I had my fun apparently, so it's over now. I crossed off the whole *what's under the kilt* thing off my bucket list."

"Fine, you win. Stop having a *whole week* of fun because… I don't know, because you're overthinking things."

"It's your job to be impulsive and mine to overthink. It's why we work."

"Honestly, I'm surprised you didn't overthink Sean."

I paused, unsure of what to say. While I was usually the first to try and talk Katie out of one of her crazy schemes, I hadn't said much about the wedding in a negative sense. I had convinced her to not dye her hair brown, compelled her out of selling her belongings and joining a commune, and advised against bungee jumping at a place that didn't seem to be up to safety code. But she had seemed too dreamily obsessed with Sean, I could hardly find fault with the guy, especially after seeing the way he looked at her.

"How did you know Sean was the one?"

Her face softened at once and she looked out over the water as she spoke. "I hate to be cliché, but when you know, you know. It was like... when I first met Sean; it was like we were the same person, but not. He keeps me grounded and I need that. And he had such a weird upbringing... like, his parents sent him to boarding school as soon as he could tie his shoes."

"Ouch." I thought of his father, who seemed nice enough when I met him briefly, but his mother was aloof, to say the least.

"I know. And their divorce was so ugly. It hurts my heart a little. He isn't great at explaining his feelings when it comes to that, but he never got to really be a kid."

"And you think you can help him have fun?"

"I hope so. But I love him, Rose. I really do and I know he feels the same way. Like when you can be completely honest and yourself without being scared they'll run away screaming, you'll know you've made the right decision."

My heart tightened with her words. I wanted her to love, to be loved, with everything in her and I knew she would. I had to. I wouldn't talk her out of her marriage because I saw and felt how happy she was. I could be practical and serious until the cows came home, but I didn't feel the need to be that person then.

She polished off her cone. "Come on, let's go do some touristy stuff and get it out of your system."

Even as we milled through the shops and stalls, filling my bags with random junk that would do little more than collect dust, my traitorous mind kept drifting over thoughts of Katie and Sean, but most of all, Lachlan.

When it came down to it, Lachlan and I got off on the wrong foot and firmly stayed there. The only reason we ended up in bed together was that we were both too drunk to realize who we were smearing blue and purple all over. It wasn't like the cosmos was throwing us together in some wacky, out-of-control series of events in which we'd ride off into the sunset like in some movie. I mean, what the hell did my life look like? A romance novel?

As if.

Chapter Five

KATIE PICKED ME up the next morning outside the hotel.
She was driving a rather nice Mercedes that was a far
cry from the used Toyota she drove at home. She beeped
loudly as I approached and I almost got into the wrong—I
mean *right* side of the car. I had momentarily forgotten that
the driver's seat was on the opposite side in the UK and only
hoped that Katie's driving lessons had gone well.

"You're going to love the castle," she said as she pulled
into traffic. "It's going to be really helpful to have you be
able to see it all so you can get a real sense of what I'm going
for and so I can get your feedback. The guest rooms are
being made ready now so the bridal party can stay over for a
few nights before and after the wedding. It'll be really great
to have everyone so close."

"That's fun. I've never been in a real castle... unless Cinderella's at Disney Land counts."

"Trust me, this castle would make Cinderella divorce her
husband for having a tiny house."

She wasn't kidding. Twenty minutes later we pulled into
the massive, walled gate and into the long drive leading

through the initial estate. Perfectly manicured lawns and a canopy of pink-blossomed trees made for a beautiful entryway. The drive was smooth and freshly paved, probably covering the stone or gravel that made up the original pathway. It was strange to think that there were, at one point, horse-drawn carriages that drove that very way just a hundred or so years ago.

An impressive, stone tower loomed over the grass and trees that surrounded the castle. The main building itself had several large structures with plenty of windows, a few short towers on the corners that probably boasted spectacular views of the grounds. I thought it might have once been a fortress, but the light stone gave it a more magical feel, as did the massive mounds of white flowers that surrounded the base.

I could see what looked like an expansive, walled garden in the back when we reached a bend in the drive, but it disappeared out of sight as we came to the front doors. They were just as remarkable as the rest, dark wood with a gargoyle on either side of the wide staircase.

To my surprise, Mattie helped us each out of the car. But I assumed he was there to help with the wedding preparations since he worked for Sean's family. Really, I was too busy staring up at the castle before me to give much thought to anything other than exploring such a historical location.

"Do you love it?" Katie asked, looping her arm through mine.

"It's fantastic."

"Come on, I'll show you everything."

We walked the same path the guests would on her wedding day, around the side of the castle and to the gardens I saw before. We went through a set of filigree, iron gates and ended up standing where the aisle would be, flanked by a line of tall hedges that made a set of walls for privacy. At the end was an open circle, which was also encased in vibrant green hedges.

"There will be chairs here and here," she explained, pointing to either side. "And we'll be hanging these little lights in the leaves so they'll glow at night when this whole space is clear for post-dinner wandering."

"It's gorgeous."

"There's also a lake all the way at the end of the gardens, but I doubt we'll really be using that."

"Where will the reception be?" I asked, peering around through my dark sunglasses. The summer day was uncharacteristically warm and I was glad I chose to wear a pale purple sundress and sandals. Otherwise, I might have melted.

"First, we'll be doing champagne and little appetizers in the main gardens and then have the sit-down dinner inside. Come on, I'll show you that next."

Something caught my eye and I stopped walking. "Is that a guy on a horse?"

"I think so. Must be Lachlan."

I was about to ask why he was at the wedding venue on horseback when he galloped towards us, stopping a few yards away. He leapt from his mount and, to my great relief, he wasn't wearing his Braveheart costume anymore. Instead, he was in a pair of jeans and plain white T-shirt that clung to his chest with sweat. Honestly, it was a shame he wasn't in a kilt to give him a real Scottish vibe.

"Good day to ye," he said, leaving his horse to graze on the immaculate grass. I eyed it nervously, wondering if the animal would harm the lawn any. I would hate for Katie to lose her deposit because the owner said Lachlan's horse ruined his backyard.

"Why are you all sweaty?" Katie asked, her nose scrunched.

He yanked the dirt-smeared shirt over his head and brushed his hair from his face. "I was makin' sure the land was sorted for the weddin' and the pens for animals secure. Good thing too, because I found quite a few chickens and sheep wanderin' where they shouldn't."

Katie glanced my way. I could see her out of the corner of my eye and she had that dumb grin on her face that she always did when she knew I was embarrassed or uncomfortable. As for Lachlan, he was steadily avoiding my gaze, choosing to stare at Katie, his horse, the castle, and a rock before even daring a peek at me. As far as I was concerned, he was doing the right thing. If he wasn't a fan of what we did, then I had no reason to bring it to his attention.

"Everythin' goin' well with the weddin'?" Lachlan finally broke the silence that had fallen over us with the topic of the upcoming nuptials. It was always a safe subject.

"Very," Katie replied. "I was just about to show Rose where we'll do dinner and dancing."

"Why don't ye let her choose her own room as well? She'll have first claim when the time comes."

"Do you think they'll be ready soon?"

He frowned a moment in thought. "Oh, aye. In fact, they'll all be ready by tomorrow for the guests. I called Sean to tell him, but he was in a meetin'."

"That soon?" Katie's voice was excited and she gripped onto my arm. "Rosie, this is going to be so much fun! This time tomorrow, we're going to be staying here. It's just like when we played princesses when we were little except instead of a tree house, we have a legit castle."

I smiled in return, trying my best to focus on her instead of the shirtless man standing by the horse. Sure, to think I'd literally had his dick in my mouth at some point, but I honestly hadn't seen Lachlan in any sort of undress while I wasn't several drinks deep and about to jump his bones. And there was a lot to appreciate. His chest was smooth and tanned; a series of trim muscles beneath his pectorals and the coat of arms tattoo showed a life of hard work, not hours in the gym, something that made sense since he was apparently the stable lad or whatever. It was a shame I didn't think he'd want to go for round two in bed.

"Come on, let's go in and you can show me where dinner will be," I prodded. Then I followed Katie towards the castle, the tenseness in my shoulders easing as we walked away from Lachlan.

"I can't believe you slept with him," she hissed as we came to a large, red, wooden door that was framed by potted white rosebushes.

"Can we *not* talk about how I banged the stable boy?"

Her forehead creased and she stopped, her hand on the iron doorknob. "The stable boy?"

"Isn't that what Lachlan is? The gardener or something?"

Her eyes bulged and then she began laughing, really laughing—the loud and shrill kind that hurt my ears. "Oh, my gosh... you think... you think he's the *stable boy*? Are you *joking*?"

"No. What's so funny?"

"Did you notice the name on the sign out front?"

"Yeah it was Colton or Caldron Castle, right?"

"Calder," she corrected. "Now, do you know Lachlan's full name? I know you saw his license."

I wracked my brain. I knew it was something Scottish and he had more than one last name, but I drew a blank. So I just guessed based on Sean's last name. "Lachlan Mackinnon?"

"Lachlan James *Calder* Mackinnon."

It clicked in my mind and I was stunned into uncharacteristic silence.

"He's the lord of the manor, you idiot. This is his castle!"

"No," I whispered. "You're messing with me."

"I'm not! He's the laird of clan Calder, through his mom's side. This is his castle, his lands… I guess I'm so used to everyone around here knowing about their family that I forgot you didn't. No one mentioned it to you?"

I shook my head, feeling embarrassed at being so clueless, but also oddly proud that I had banged a laird. It was like my vagina was suddenly a fancy bitch. "I had no idea. I just thought he was a *Braveheart* enthusiast."

"Well I guess he could be, since William Wallace is like his great-great-great-whatever uncle or something." She shrugged and pulled open the door that led inside. "Let's keep moving before you die of shock."

I trailed behind her into the castle, trying to push back the fact that Lachlan was Scottish nobility. It wasn't my business who he was, especially since I wasn't going to have any form of friendship with him other than whatever pleasantries I needed to exchange with him during the wedding. But I did feel a little weird that I was standing in his house—well, *castle*—and was going to even be sleeping there.

"Okay," Katie started, back in wedding-mode. "The guests will come in through here, the doors will be open already, and then cross through this entryway and down this hall."

I looked around at the deep green walls that surrounded me, the walls covered in gold-framed paintings of people in kilts, on horseback, and wearing fabulous jewels. Worn, polished, wood made up the floor beneath my feet and I followed Katie down the hall, which was covered in a long, Oriental carpet. We passed more paintings and several closed doors, until we came to the pavilion.

The room was large and airy, lit by a series of windows that let in copious amounts of natural sunlight. Circular tables enclosed a decently-sized dance floor that sat beneath a gorgeous chandelier. It felt almost modern there, a stark difference to the classical vibe that I got on my way in.

"Each table is going to have candles, vines, white roses… it'll be gorgeous," Katie told me excitedly. "I'm going to have these super light blue tablecloths and we'll be putting a great dessert bar in the back of the room for after dinner."

"It's going to be beautiful. I can't believe there are only four more days before the wedding."

"I know! They're going to start prepping this room in the morning, I think. So, come on. Let's go snatch you up a room before Sean's family take the good ones."

I doubted the castle had any bad rooms, but nodded and fell into step beside her. We went back into the entryway we had first came into and then rounded a corner into what I could only describe as the grand entryway. Double, vaulted ceilings encased an impressive, dark wood staircase that wound upwards to the next level. The walls were exposed stone that I assumed made up the original, tall tower I had seen when we drove in. A giant Calder clan crest sat on the wall in a place of honor, flanked by faded tapestries that must have been ancient.

"Wow." My word was soft, but it echoed in the space.

"I know. I could die."

"How old is this place?"

She shrugged and then paused thoughtfully. "I forget exactly when, but I think Sean said this tower was built somewhere in the twelfth century and then there were additions made throughout. Lachlan's also slowly modernizing parts of it, like the bathrooms and all that."

I thought it was a shame to modernize any of the castle, but then the thought of using a chamber pot was enough to make me gag and I immediately supported his decision. Katie began to climb the stairs and I shook my head before following, trying to process all that I saw.

I wondered what lords and ladies had walked the same path and ran my hand over the stones. The view from the second floor overlooking the entryway was just as nice, but Katie gave me little time to appreciate it, as she began dragging me down the hallway. Again, they were lined with countless paintings and portraits that I made mental notes to take a closer look at when I didn't have Katie rushing me around. I could be passing work made by famous artists.

"Okay, I think you should go in the blue room," she told me, leading me to the end of one long hall lined with doors. "It has a private bathroom and overlooks the gardens."

"Sounds good to me."

She opened the door to reveal a spacious room with

white and blue striped walls and two large, arched windows framed by thick royal-blue curtains. There was a four-poster bed with blue velvet bedding, and fresh white roses sat in a vase on the dresser. I saw the bathroom, as the door was open, beside a large wardrobe that looked old enough and big enough to be a secret entryway to Narnia.

"Nice. I'll take it," I said, crossing the room to look out one of the windows.

The gardens were below as Katie promised, but something else caught my eye. Lachlan stood among the perfectly manicured bushes below. His horse was nowhere to be seen, but his abs were on full display as he talked with someone who appeared to be an actual gardener. In that moment, I thought it was a crying shame he still wasn't wearing a kilt, but I would never admit it out loud.

"Like the view?" Katie asked over my shoulder.

I hadn't heard her come up behind me.

My cheeks heated and I turned away from the window. "Shut up, Kathryn."

"Only if you admit that you're sorry you only slept with him when drunk and not fully able to appreciate that hot Scot shot of whisky."

"Well, I know I'm sorry I got caught by you."

"You would have told me eventually."

"Maybe, maybe not."

"You have to tell me these things more than ever now."

"Why?"

"Because I'll be an old married lady. I need to live through you!"

I rolled my eyes. "Then you'll be sorely disappointed."

"Ah, I thought I'd find you both here!" Sean appeared in the doorway behind us, looking much cleaner than his cousin in a red polo and jeans.

"Hey, I thought I was going to meet you later," Katie said as she went to kiss him.

"Lachlan called to tell me everyone could move in to-morrow and I wanted to see how things were coming along with the wedding," he explained. "Then when I saw your car here, I thought it might be nice for the four of us to dine together in town."

"The four of us?" I asked, even though I knew what he was talking about.

Sean smiled. "Yourself, Lachlan, Kathryn, and me."

"That sounds like a great idea!" She had that dumb grin on her face again. "Right, Rosie Posey?"

"Of course, Katie Cat," I said tightly.

Unfortunately, I couldn't think of a way out of it. It wasn't like I could lie and say I had other plans. Katie was the only one I even knew in Scotland.

"Splendid. Then let's retire to the library until Lachlan is ready to join us."

Sean turned from the room then, taking Katie's hand. We went downstairs and through a small door off to one side in the entryway. It led us into a library, one wall of shelves filled with leather and canvas volumes covered one wall. There was also a small fireplace that looked as old as the tower, the stone around it was worn smooth and parts were blackened from decades of use. A comfortable-looking green couch and a matching armchair flanked a large, oak desk. It was almost surprising to see a laptop sitting closed on the top, but it just reminded me that I wasn't back in time, but in my own.

"Cozy, isn't it?" Sean asked as he sat down on the couch beside Katie.

"It's magnificent."

I peered at some of the book titles and saw many of the classics. But the spines looked worn and well used, not like a series of volumes bought for show, and I wondered if Lachlan had been the one to scuff the spines. Or it was also possible that the books had always been there, brought in by past residents. That seemed more likely.

Then the library door opened and Lachlan stood there dressed in a pale green button-down. Sadly, no kilt again, but it wasn't like I had the right to be really disappointed.

"Is everyone ready?" Lachlan was rolling his sleeves up to his elbows, making him look even more like a model than he already did.

"Where shall we go?" Sean asked him. "Down to *McGillian's*?"

Lachlan shook his head. "I thought we might try *The Ruins*. I've heard good things."

"Then you drive, aye?"

"O' course."

Then we all filed out to the front of the castle, where a dark grey Range Rover sat running. Lachlan took the front driver's seat while Katie and Sean filled in the back. That left me in the copilot position. I thought it might give me a chance to make some polite small talk with him and wash away some of the awkwardness. If we could just raise ourselves above everything, we could erase… well, every time we had been in the same room together.

"So what's *The Ruins*?" I asked as Lachlan began the long journey down the drive.

"You'll love it," Sean promised, ruining my plan to have Lachlan be the one to explain things. "It's a terribly exclusive restaurant. Waiting lists are very long for a table."

That didn't make sense to me. If this was some top of the line place, how could we just go there on a whim? "Then how will we get in?"

Lachlan laughed quietly and said, "Good point, hold on." He pressed a button on the futuristic center console and the sound of a phone ringing filled the Range Rover.

A woman with a soft, British accent answered. "Good evening, you have reached *The Ruins*, how may I help you?"

"Hello, Jane, it's Lachlan."

"Oh, hello!" The woman sounded flustered, like she had forgotten how to talk on the phone. "Would you care to book a table, sir?"

"Aye, I would. I'll be there in twenty minutes with three guests."

"Very good sir. We'll be expecting you."

Click!

I blinked, surprised at the short exchange that had just occurred. "What was that?"

"I own a bit o' stock in this particular establishment," he explained, his eyes still on the road.

"Like as a backer?"

Katie pulled out her phone and began tapping away. "Now I'm curious. Are we underdressed? Rose and I are just in sundresses and you're in jeans."

"You look lovely," Sean affirmed as he slipped the phone out of her hand and back into her purse. "Just wait and see. This surprise will be well worth it."

I looked out the window, where the sun was just beginning to set below the rolling hills we passed. It lit the sky in a vivid stream of orange and red with purple streaks. I waited to see the lights of a city approach us, but it seemed as if we were going farther into the country. But I wasn't familiar enough with the area to really know where.

"Do ye see it?" Lachlan asked me quietly. "There between those two mounds?"

I did. Rising up from the ground like homage to the past, *The Ruins* had been aptly named. It was apparently the skeleton of some ancient castle, half gone with age. The outside of the rough, stone building was imposing and dark in the dying sun, but seemed to be glowing softly from the inside like some kind of stone jack-o-lantern. Spots of light poured from small, slit-like windows and pooled on the lawn. It sat some distance off the road we were driving on, and I realized that was what the Range Rover was for.

"Hold on," Lachlan ordered. Then he turned harshly to the left, steering the vehicle over the uneven ground.

I bounced in my seat and gripped the door as he drove. "Why isn't there a road?"

"Because this is no' a permanent structure in that sense. It's no' meant to be a true restaurant."

"Then what is it?"

"A piece o' history."

When we pulled up to the entrance of *The Ruins*, where the door was just the stone frame, a valet came to collect us instantly. The few cars around us were high-end vehicles, foreign and classic alike. In my pale purple dress and sandals, I figured we wouldn't even make it inside.

"Good evening, Mr. Mackinnon." A woman I assumed was Jane greeted us beneath the archway. "Your table is just through here."

We walked single file behind her and I swear I felt a chill up my spine. It was the most remarkable place I'd ever seen, like the kind of place one imagined might exist, but knew it didn't. But there I was, standing between the walls of what must have once been a mighty fortress of the Highlands. It had no roof, just the strong walls and a single tower. Above us was the blackening sky and below us sat just grass and the remnants of rock that might have fallen from the ceiling centuries ago.

Only a dozen white-clothed tables sat inside the castle's skeleton. Each was lit by several candles in the center of each, which surrounded black vases of perfect, blood-red roses. There was no music; save for the sound of the summer crickets and my mind couldn't understand where we were. Why was there a restaurant there? Who were these people? Was there a high-tech kitchen beneath our feet?

Sean helped Katie into her seat, while Lachlan did the same for me, despite my protests that I could do it myself. No one offered us a menu for food or drinks, but just filled our glass goblets with ice water in one and red wine in the other.

"Wow, this is fantastic," Katie said, her eyes darting around in the same way mine probably were.

"Isn't it?" Sean agreed.

"We should have had our wedding here… no offence, Lachlan."

He took a sip of his wine and smiled. "None taken. If I could allow ye to do that without harmin' this space, I would. But my home is better suited to your needs."

"Oh, I know. It's just… so amazing. Wait… If *you* could allow it?"

"Well, it's my castle," he said simply as a pair of waiters in suits came over and put four colorful salads before us.

"How many castles do you own?" I asked before I could stop myself.

"Just the two. This and my residence."

"But there's the Italian one as well," Sean pointed out as if he wasn't talking about actual historic architecture. "Well, perhaps it's not appropriate to call it a castle. It's more of a villa."

"That belongs to the family."

"Why make it a restaurant?" I asked, wishing I could see the grand building in the light of day. "I don't know much about old places, but wouldn't hosting a bunch of people here like this really mess up this place?"

"No, in fact, the guests here are what's keepin' this place still standin'," he explained to me as I began eating my salad. "Ye see, although this is basically crumbled with time, it's only recently come to my attention how bad it's become. In order to keep the tower standin', it needed to be reinforced, but correctly as to no' take away from the original architecture."

"So you opened it up for guests?"

"Aye, just a limited number, on limited weekends, with a limited menu."

"Where is everything cooked?"

He laughed. "Do ye really want to know?"

"Obviously."

"Trucks."

Katie's eyes grew wide. "Trucks?"

Sean nodded. "Behind the castle, a series of food trucks are lined up. That way, the castle doesn't need to be altered."

I was shocked that the meals came from food trucks. The wine was fruity and earthy, the silverware polished to a perfect shine. The rack of lamb was exquisite, at least I thought so since it wasn't like I ate a lot of lamb in New Jersey. The potatoes and rolls served alongside were perfect as well. And by the time the dessert of baked apples over freshly churned ice cream was served, I was firmly in love with the Highlands.

Drunk on wine and good food, it was easy to forget that I had an uncomfortable moment with Lachlan. He seemed good-natured in the yellow-tinted light of the candles on the table. The lines of his face were softened and he smiled more often than not. It was nice to see him in his natural habitat, relaxed and playing the part of the perfect host. Gone was the look of indifferent scorn I thought I had seen that morning in my hotel room. I liked it.

"If no one's in a rush to leave, I'd like to bring ye all too see somethin'," Lachlan announced when our dessert dishes were cleared.

We all stood and followed him to the back of the ruins, to a door opposite the one we entered. It let us out to the back of the castle and there was a small line of food trucks in the near distance, their generators humming in the quiet of the night. I thought he'd take us to the trucks, since there was nothing out there besides the hills, but we ended up skirting the wall until we were beside the base of the tower.

"Is anyone afraid o' heights?" he asked, pulling out a single, small key from his pocket. The light of the stars showed a small door, obviously a new installation, which he promptly unlocked.

Lachlan entered the dark stairway first and I followed. It was pitch-black, save for the random slit-windows that dotted the spiral staircase. I ran my fingers over the wall as we climbed, feeling the age seep into my hands. I loved the feeling of so much history, but I couldn't dwell too much, as we soon reached our destination.

The platform atop the tower was small, but had enough space for all of us to stand comfortably, all by the crumbling edges that separated us from the three-story fall. Below I could see the candles making the whites of the tablecloths glow and felt the wind from the mountains skim over my skin and through my hair. I closed my eyes and breathed deeply. I've heard people say they could taste the air and know where they were, and I had never understood that until now.

In that moment, under the canopy of a cloudless, starlit sky, when Katie reached over and took my hand in hers, I didn't care about anything else in the world. I didn't care about my awkwardness over the ruined kilt, or how the morning after my one-night stand was uncomfortable, or even that I only had a few days left in Scotland. Because, for the first time in a long time, I felt like I was where I was meant to be and I wouldn't let anyone ruin it.

Chapter Six

THE NEXT AFTERNOON, Katie and I dragged our suitcases out of the car, with the help of Sean. He stacked our bags beside the front doors and a man came out and began to bring them inside. I was starting to get used to the star treatment in Scotland and I wasn't really looking forward to having to lug my own shit around when I got home.

"Are we dressing for dinner?" Katie asked Sean as he closed the car's trunk.

"Aye, I believe so. But not terribly formal," he replied, tucking one of her bouncy red curls behind her ear. "I'm sure whatever you wear will be lovely."

"Thank you, future husband. What do you have planned now?"

"I thought I'd go down to the gardens to see where the staff was in the preparations. The lights should all be placed by now and I wanted to ensure the fountain in the west is in working order."

"I think I'll join you." She turned to me. "Rosie, do you want to come?"

I shook my head, not feeling like encroaching on their

lovefest. "No, thanks. I think I'm going to head up and shower and get settled, if that's okay."

Katie nodded. "Okay, I'll come and get you for dinner around seven thirty."

I was looking forward to looking around a bit on my way to my room and inhaled deeply when I entered through the large double doors that led me into the grand entryway. The wood and stone that made up hundreds of years of history invited me in and I wished I could explore more of the castle, but didn't want to get caught snooping around in Lachlan's house.

The night before ended on a positive note, where we were dropped off at Katie's car and she and I returned to the hotel. She was in such a good mood, she didn't even tease me about Lachlan or complain her wedding wasn't going to be in some fabulous ruins. Lachlan and I were even keeping our personal feelings of uncomfortable closeness in check, apparently choosing to ignore our little fling.

So I took my time going upstairs, looking into the face of each portrait I passed and even daring to touch some tapestries and decorative vases as I went... when I was sure there wasn't anyone around to see. There was even a large ax on one wall that I hadn't noticed before, but the double blades looked wickedly sharp and I had no interest in poking it. It was strange to see weapons used as decoration. At home, I would never tape my pepper spray to the wall and call it art.

My room looked the same as the day before, but with my

bags beside the bed and fresh pink roses in place of the white on the dresser. I gave them a small sniff. Pink roses were my favorite and having them paired with a few nights in a historic castle seemed too good to be true. I could hardly believe I was soon going to be watching my best friend in the world getting married at such an amazing location and wondered if I could get her to take me on a proper tour before the wedding.

The bathroom was thankfully modern with granite countertops and bright lights framing a large mirror that would be perfect for my makeup applications. I took a long shower, knowing I had more than two hours before Katie would come to collect me, and emerged feeling relaxed and refreshed.

I wasn't sure what dressing for dinner entailed, but Sean said it wasn't terribly formal. Still, when someone said anything about changing their outfits just to eat, I knew they assumed I had more class to not show up in jeans. So I pulled out a grey, sleeveless, jersey wrap dress where the hem hit just above my knees that made me look like the former Kate Middleton, the current Duchess of Cambridge.

I was just finishing the final touches on my makeup when there was a knock on my door. Katie stood in the hall, wearing the exact same dress as me, only in rose petal pink. We stared at each other for a few moments before bursting into laughter. We did almost all of our shopping together in New Jersey and often ended up buying similar or matching things. While it wasn't an uncommon occurrence, it was still funny when it happened.

"Even in another country we can't help but wear the same stuff," I said. "Want me to change?"

"No way. I told everyone we were basically the same person, this only highlights it."

I thought about what she said as we started down towards the dining room. In reality, we were the farthest thing from twins. She was red haired, rosy cheeked, with brown eyes, a thin build. On the other hand, my hair was dark as night, my eyes a pale blue grey, and I sported enough curves for the both of us. But as far as our personalities, sense of humor and—since I slept with Sean's cousin—our taste in men went, we could pass as more than just sorority sisters.

"You'll love the dining room," she said as we strode down the darkened corridors. "It has all that old stuff you obsess over."

"Oh, you mean your future family's old stuff?"

Katie rolled her eyes as we got to the landing at the bottom of the stairs and led me down a hallway I hadn't gone down before. "You know what I mean."

She was right. The dining room was cozy, but elaborate. The deep red walls soaked in the glow of the candles that lined the long table that was set with four places. Each one boasted several forks for different courses, just like the table the night before. Framed oil paintings of birds sat on either side of the room and stuffed ducks and pheasants were mounted between them. As I took a closer look at the table, I saw that sprigs of heather were tucked beneath each candle as a delicate decoration.

"I was right," Sean said from the doorway, surprising both Katie and me. "You do look lovely in anything."

"Aw, thank you!" Katie immediately latched onto him and I wondered if that was what it was like to be completely, ridiculously in love with someone. If one held onto them like a mechanical bull at a dive bar—tightly and to the point of breaking a bone, scared they might die if one let go.

Lachlan entered behind Sean. His dark blond hair looked wet as if he had just showered and he wore a white button-down shirt with the sleeves rolled up to the elbow. And, to my secret pleasure, he also had on a kilt. Not a *Braveheart*-esque one, but the modern blues and greens of his clan. I thought it odd that Sean chose some slacks instead, but assumed it was a preference thing.

"Shall we sit?" Sean asked, leading Kate to her place on one side of the table.

I went to sit beside her, but then Lachlan was there, pulling out my chair and helping me push it into the table. My cheeks flamed, but I didn't know why. After all, I supposed it was his gentlemanly duty as lord of *Downton Abbey* to be old school.

"Thank you," I muttered, busying myself with unfolding the crisp white napkin onto my lap.

Sean sat down across from Katie and Lachlan was across

from me. For a moment, our eyes locked and a zap of electricity travelled through my body, leaving me feeling like I had just done something against the rules.

Thankfully, a woman entered, who identified herself as the cook. She gave us the menu for the evening; smoked salmon and asparagus then some kind of soup called a "Cullen skink" that I hope tasted better than it sounded. For the main course there would be venison and roast vegetables, followed by dessert. A footman entered when she left, filling our cups, one with ice water, the other with chilled white wine.

"How are you finding your accommodations?" Sean asked me politely as the first course was placed before us.

"Wonderful. Katie put me in the blue room."

"The one by Lachlan's?" he enquired with a quick, sideways look in her direction. "I suppose that is a rather fine room."

Katie was looking intently at her asparagus. "It has a lovely view of the garden. By the way, the gardens looked amazing, Lachlan. The staff did a wonderful job."

Lachlan smiled over the rim of his wineglass. "I'm glad to hear it. The weather calls for rain in the early evening tomorrow, but then they'll be able to set up the chairs and some other odds and ends."

The conversation flowed easily around the topic of the wedding and before I knew it, the plates had all been cleared and glass dishes of raspberry cranachan put before us. The sweet, fruity, oat mixture was odd, but not in a bad way. I tasted strong notes of honey whisky between the layers of cream and berries that, in my head, had been picked that morning somewhere in the forest that surrounded the castle.

"I'm stuffed," Katie groaned a little bit later, pushing her cup away. "I can't believe I'm eating like this before I need to fit into my gown, especially after last night."

"It was perfect, wasn't it?" Sean agreed.

"Yes. I can't believe you hid it from me."

"I wanted it to be a surprise, Lachlan merely expedited the situation. Now, shall we tour the gardens, then?"

"Aye, we should," Lachlan said. "We can see the full effects of the lights in the hedges. Then Kathryn can decide if it's to her likin' so we can make any adjustments."

"I bet it's going to be beautiful!" Katie rose from her seat and took Sean's arm and yanked him up immediately. They began leading the way out of the dining room while I was still untangling the feet of chair from the long tablecloth that had somehow gotten wound around the leg.

"Here, let me help." Lachlan was by my side and crouched down, untangling whatever had caused my problem.

"Thank you," I said as he pulled back the chair, giving me my freedom. My eyes darted towards the door, but Katie and Sean were gone. I couldn't even hear their footsteps on the hard floor.

"They'll be in the garden now. Sean knows how to turn

on the fairy lights."

We strode at a distance from the dining room, down a slim corridor, and into the pavilion. At one point he was so close, I could almost touch him, but obviously didn't. I wanted nothing more than to find Katie and be back in her safe company where I was sure I wouldn't get into any more trouble. There was still a lot of guilt surrounding what I had done to the kilt and my one night with Lachlan had done little to quell my feelings. In fact, they intensified the fact I didn't think he liked me all that much.

When we stepped outside in full view of the garden, it had been transformed in the darkness. The hedges and trees were draped in white fairy lights, causing an extension of the full, starlit sky above that seemingly stretched on, into the hills. The air was so still and fragrant with the specific scent of freshness that one could only ever get in the country... but still, no Katie.

"Where is she?" I asked myself quietly.

"Knowin' my cousin, they're off hidin' in the stables or maybe out by the wee greenhouse on the far end o' the estate."

I didn't expect him to answer, but he was probably right. Katie and Sean were long gone and I wouldn't see her again until the next day. "I guess I should go up to my room then."

"You do no' wish to see the rest?"

"I don't want to impose."

"I do no' bite, Rose. Come out with me. Ye can no' say we're strangers."

He had a point. I couldn't say someone was a stranger when I'd had their dick in my mouth. That would just make me a liar. And I was a great many things, but not one of those.

I fell into step beside him and we entered the walled gardens through the intricate iron gate. It opened silently, but closed behind us with a loud clang, making me jump. He looked over at me, his face lit by tiny, white lights, one brow raised in amusement.

"Do no' fret so. The only ghost in the castle is a very kind one."

"Ghosts? You're joking."

"No, I never joke about my ancestors."

"Yeah? Then who is this super nice, ancestral ghost?" I asked, milling around the small bushes and tufts of pink and purple flowers.

He didn't follow me, but leaned back against the leafy wall, watching me. "It's a long-gone Lady Calder who is said to watch over the guests within the castle."

"A fan of hospitality, was she?"

"The best kind o' hostess. I promise, ye'll have the best nights o' sleep under my roof, for she will look in on ye."

His words processed and I turned to face him. I had forgotten that I was a guest in his *home*, and not just staying in some themed hotel. The castle wasn't just a wedding venue, but where he lived. It was intimate in a way I wasn't accustomed to.

"Thank you for having me to stay," I said politely, not looking directly at him, but at a climbing vine that curled beside his head.

"I'm surprised you agreed to."

"What? Why wouldn't I?"

"To say we got off on the wrong foot would be a massive understatement."

"I guess I *did* ruin a family heirloom… which I'm still fully prepared to pay for, by the way. I even hit up an ATM at the hotel and have cash in my wallet for it right now. I can go up to get my room and—"

"The kilt? Ye mean from the welcome party?"

Unable to speak, I just nodded and hoped the lights weren't bright enough to show my expression. I couldn't tell from his tone if he was angry with me for bringing it up again. Either way, I held my breath.

His mouth split into a grin and then he laughed aloud. It echoed against the walls and into the sky. "Are ye still worryin' about that?"

"It was a family heirloom," I replied, severely confused.

"No, it was no' a family heirloom, ye daft lass. Christ, I thought ye had a sense o' humor."

The heat of shame turned to one of anger as I realized he was having a good chuckle over me freaking out about dumping a bunch of burgers on him. That asshole. "What do you mean, it wasn't a family heirloom? You literally said it had been in your family for years."

"Christ," he repeated, pushing off the wall and crossing towards me. "Kathryn told me that ye adored practical jokes and dry humor. I thought… well, I thought we'd have a good laugh over it. I thought ye'd find it… funny."

"Funny? That was cruel joke to play on someone you just met. Are you deranged?"

"It's no' my fault ye do no' understand sarcasm and took it all to heart."

I gritted my teeth, not understanding how I was possibly in the wrong. "And it's not my fault that when a total stranger tells me I ruined a cultural heirloom that symbolizes generations of family ties, I believe them!" I turned on my heel in a huff, angry with Katie and Lachlan equally. While I was sure Katie had no idea he was lying about the kilt, she had still unknowingly set me up for failure by basically inviting him to try and trick a stranger.

"Rose, wait!"

But I didn't turn. I stalked through the perfectly mani-cured garden and out a small gate on the opposite side from the castle. His heavy steps followed behind me, but I was too embarrassed and angry to face him. If there was one thing I hated, it was being made to look like an idiot, especially after I tried to fix it and he blew me off.

I stopped walking when I hit the tree line on the edge of the grounds and rounded on him. Stupid garden mazes.

"Why are you following me?"

"Because it's a few miles to the next house in this direction and Kathryn would be rather vexed if I let her best friend die in the wilderness of Scotland or fall into a lake and drown and miss the weddin'."

I didn't respond, but just stared at his shape in the darkness, knowing he was right that I would probably get lost, but also wanting him to leave me the hell alone so I could stew in peace. And at the same time, I wanted to put it all behind us and just move on.

"I'm sorry, Rose," he finally said. "I made a joke and did no' know it would be ill received. I took it too far then I did no' know how to right it and before long, things got so strange. Instead of bein' a man about the whole thing, I just froze. I would never wish to be at odds with ye and I hope we can move past this, as I promise I'll never lie and say ye've destroyed a priceless heirloom again."

"I appreciate your apology."

"Might we start fresh?"

He sounded so sincere that I smiled, feeling as if a heavy, plaid weight had been lifted off my chest. "I would like that."

"I'm glad to hear it. I thought ye'd warm to me last night, but ye hardly looked my way."

"How could I? I thought I murdered a piece of Scottish history and then there was the hen party and—" My cheeks flamed. I didn't mean to bring it up, but it just slipped and then it was out there, floating between us.

"Aye, I suppose we need to clear the air on that account as well."

"I guess so."

"I... I usually don't do that, Rose. Sleep with a woman like that, I mean. Ye know, without doin' it properly and... then I saw ye, but I did no'..."

"I'm not following you."

"What I mean to say is that when I saw ye in the disco—"

"You knew that was me?" I cut in.

"O' course. Ye were wearin' a wee crown on your head, no' a paper bag. Things just went so quickly in the mornin' and I had a ragin' headache and I knew I looked a right fool, all trussed up like that."

"So you ran out of my room and refused to make eye contact with me like I was Medusa because you had a headache?"

"I mean to say that I didn't know what came next and I... I panicked, Rose." He raked a hand through his hair, making it stand on end. "Christ, I thought I was a smart man, but I made a dumb decision. I thought that a castle or two would right things, but you're a tough woman to please. Shall I take ye to another to ensure ye smile once in a while?"

I couldn't help but do just that, especially after his confession. Everything I had thought soured things between us was just in my head. There was a definite downside to being a chronic overthinker, besides the fact that I was sometimes so wrapped up in my own shit, I couldn't see the forest through the trees.

"If I get to meet a royal, I'll let it slide," I said.

"I can call my third cousin, Roger. He's a British lord, if that counts."

"Direct royal line, or nothing."

Lachlan laughed and shook his head. "I'll see what I can do."

We stood together in silence, overlooking his ancestral homeland. The gardens were glowing and some windows in the castle shone out to the yard. It was a gorgeous sight and I couldn't imagine actually living there, knowing it was my home and the light that spilled across the lawns and gardens were echoes of life from *my* family and friends. I wanted to ask Lachlan if it felt real. If he entered those doors after time away and thought, *I'm home*, and was filled with the sensation of familiarity and coziness that embraced me when I came home to my apartment after following a firm partner to a weekend conference. But it wouldn't be polite to ask such a personal question.

It was weird that I would feel so awkward and out of place next to someone I had slept with. We had touched and kissed almost every part of each other, spent the night in each other's arms. But I had been calling him William Wallace and had to sneak a peek in his wallet the next morning; it doesn't really count.

"What's so funny?" he asked, breaking me from my

thoughts.

"What?"

"You're smilin' somethin' fierce."

"Was I?"

"Aye, like I had just charmed ye with one o' my jokes."

"No more jokes. You remember how the last one turned out."

"Don't fret. I've learned my lesson," he promised. "Shall we go back down, now?"

I nodded and we slowly walked towards the gate we had so recently slipped from. The path felt different though, with the stress finally gone, and we were only maybe a breath away from one another. If I wanted to, I could move my hand and entwine my fingers with his... not that I wanted to, of course.

"It's so peaceful here," I whispered as we paused beside a large fountain off to one side of the garden. The pool beneath was filled with flowing lilies and water cascaded from basins held aloft by angels.

"Aye, it is. I come out here sometimes when I wish to be alone."

"Do you wish you were alone now?" I regretted saying it as soon as the words were out there. It sounded suggestive somehow. But there was no turning back.

He seemed surprised by my question. "Alone? Why would I wish that? I mean, sometimes solitude is a fillin' thing to take in, but sometimes... sometimes being alone is too much to bear."

"I know that feeling. After Katie and Sean get married, I won't have anyone." Tears pricked my eyelids and I willed them back down. I had already looked stupid in front of Lachlan so many times, I would drown myself in the fountain before I let it happen again.

"Ye'll have your visits and all that."

"Sometimes that's not enough. We've done everything together for years and now I'll have to do things alone. I guess I need to find my own fountain of solitude back in New Jersey."

"A place ye can go for a wee bit o' peace is a fine thing to have."

He seemed to have stepped closer to me, but I couldn't decide if it was just a figment of my imagination. The pressure between us was so thick; I could cut it with a knife. It was like a scene in a movie where the couple finally met and had their dramatic kiss in a beautiful location after refusing their true desires for so long...

So, obviously, my idiot mouth decided to get sassy and ruin everything. "You know, you look a lot different when you're not dressed up like a historically inaccurate cosplayer."

Lachlan stared at me a moment then burst out in raucous laughter. "Well, *you* look a lot more bonny when you're no' dressed like a drunken fairy and fallin' off the bed."

"Hey, I'm an absolute delight when I'm drunk. Besides, I didn't hear any complaining on your end."

"And ye would never... no' that ye likely remember much, in any case."

"I have a flawless memory."

"Enough o' a memory to remember my name so well, ye had to go rootin' through my wallet to find out?"

I flushed, but wasn't completely embarrassed. I was filled with the rush of expectation that followed that familiar dance. We were on the cusp of the game men and women play where they toss teases back and forth, seeing who would be the one to stop the witty banter and get down to business.

Turned out, Lachlan was the weaker link. He bent low and, before I could form an idea in my head of what was going to happen, he kissed me. One hand rested on my lower back, the other cupped my cheek. His lips were soft and warm, but filled with underlying need that pulsed through me. His mouth tasted like the honeyed raspberries we had for dessert and I drew my body closer, slowly reaching a hand up to touch his arm and slid it upwards to his shoulder and neck.

When he broke the kiss, we didn't fully separate. "I've been waitin' to do that sober."

"Were you?"

He nodded, moving back from me and taking my hand in his. "Since I first saw ye in the deep, red dress at the party. And even more so when I saw that shocked look on your face over the plaid."

I rolled my eyes and he squeezed my fingers. "Ugh, I

never want to talk about that again."

"You're right. I said I would no' tease ye, but it's so hard no' to."

"I have faith in you that you'll be able to stop."

"I may be in need o' a wee bit o' encouragement in the matter."

"Is that so?"

He pulled me to him again, pressing me hard against his chest. It was so strange how we had been so close a few nights before, and I still felt as if we had just kissed for the first time. The urgency of newness filled me and I relished in the sensation I hadn't known in so long. The other chaste, first date kisses with my dates back in Jersey seemed mechanical and perfunctory in comparison.

When he kissed me again, I leaned into his lips. If I still wanted to have a fleeting lust affair with a hot Scottish guy, Lachlan was more than fitting for the job. He spread a fire through my veins that left me breathless, and although his hands stayed neatly on my back and waist, I wanted him to explore my curves so I could feel his fingers on my bare skin. I wanted the gentleman of the castle to become the rugged Highlander I desperately craved.

My arms looped around his neck and I opened my mouth at the beckoning of his tongue. The gardens were secluded enough for an evening tryst and I wondered how far we could get. His body felt so good against mine and I wanted to experience it—*really* experience it—without the hazy, dark fog of alcohol clouding my mind.

But then the lights went out all at once, plunging us into a thick darkness that even the stars above could barely cut through. Now, I wasn't an easily startled person, but I had watched enough horror movies in my lifetime to know that when a person was at an ancient castle, about to get busy with a hot guy, the ghosts of past residents were going to cock-block them… and maybe even trap them in a dungeon and steal their soul.

"Is there a dungeon here?" I asked quietly, still clinging to his shirt.

He nipped at my neck, seemingly unbothered by the situation. "No… why?"

"No reason."

"I don't know why the lights are off here. Those in the castle are still on. Come, we should go in now. I need to find out what caused this so it doesn't happen on the weddin' day."

An uncomfortable silence fell over us as we entered the pavilion, went through the halls, up the grand staircase to the second floor, and into the long hallway that was lined with doors. We came to a stop at the mouth of my room and just stood there. I wondered if I was supposed to invite him into my room or if that would be weird since it was technically *his* room and I was just borrowing it.

"You didn't have to walk me all the way up here," I said, trying to lighten the mood.

"I wasn't. My room's on the left, there."

My stomach twisted in the sickening way it usually did when I said something stupid. "Oh, yeah. I forgot."

"Kathryn thought ye'd be better suited beside me, apparently."

"I had no idea. She just picked it."

"I would expect nothin' less from her," he replied dryly.

"Well… I guess I should get into bed…."

"Are ye doin' anythin' tomorrow, Rose?"

His question caught me off guard for some reason and I immediately blanked on whatever wedding thing I was supposed to do with Katie. "Um… I think I'm supposed to go to the florist or something in the morning maybe…"

"Then would ye like to join me for lunch when ye return?"

"Sure—I mean, yes."

"Will ye be back here by one o'clock?"

"I believe so."

"Good. Thought it was the least I could do, seein' as I did no' call ye after, well… *ye know.*" Lachlan's lips curled into a smirk. "But in my defense, I technically *did* take ye to dinner." He was teasing me again, but I liked it. We were back to playing the game.

"Nope, I think you still owe me," I replied, opening up my door.

For a swift second, I almost wanted to grab him by the kilt and yank him in after me, but I was a goddamn lady…

when I wasn't full of top-shelf tequila. "So make tomorrow worth my while."

I left him standing in the hallway and smiled to myself as my door clicked shut behind me. I waited, standing still, until I heard his shoes on the wooden floor and the sounds of him going into his own bedroom. I let out the breath I had been holding and fought the urge to squeal. Now, I'd done my fair share of dating in my life, but had never gone to lunch with a Scottish lord.

I crossed the room to where my phone sat on the rosewood nightstand and slid it open. There was one unread text on the screen. It was from Katie and it said, *"You're welcome."*

Chapter Seven

INSTEAD OF THE florist, Katie and I ended up at the spa and salon, getting prepped for the big day. She left the white blooms to her mother to sort out, which was for the best, since her mom could be a little nuts when it came to planning events. It was better that she had a job to do so her need for control didn't spill into areas Katie actually cared about.

Our appointments began at seven in the morning, which felt ridiculously early, but we had a list of treatments to go through. We were passed mimosas as soon as we entered through the doors and handed fluffy, white robes and slippers. Between mouthfuls of fresh fruits, we were massaged, steamed, and waxed within an inch of our lives. By the time we were at the final appointment of the morning, our nails, we were sitting in matching chairs with our faces covered in some kind of seaweed and ash mixture that oddly smelled like lavender.

We both got our usual formal event colors, which we had down to a science after years of weddings, grad parties, and job interviews. The perfect pink shade was one coat of *Ballet*

Slippers followed by one coat of *Mademoiselle*, both by Essie. The only difference in our matching routine was that Katie also had her nails coated in a glitter powder that would complement the giant rock on her hand.

"I need one of these in my house," Katie murmured as we sat in the massage chairs during our pedicures.

"Mm-hm." I was terribly ticklish and was trying my hardest to keep it together while the nail artist buffed, polished, painted, and primed my toes.

"So... lunch with Lachlan, huh?"

"Yep. Just lunch."

"A little afternoon delight?"

I shot her a dirty look, but she only grinned. "We're just going to get something to eat. No big deal."

"I guess it isn't, since you've already slept together. What are you going to wear?"

I shrugged, trying to sort through the rest of the outfits I had brought with me to Scotland. I hadn't thought to ask where we'd be going, but it was a nice enough day, if not a little on the cool side with a slight overcast. It was crazy how the weather shifted and changed from one hour to the next. "Not sure. Any ideas?"

"You're always free to raid my closet," she offered, blowing lightly on her nails. "Did he tell you where he was taking you?"

"No, and I didn't remember to even ask."

"Then you need to be dressed nicely, but not like you're

trying too hard."

"I'm not trying anything. This is all just for a little bit of fun."

She laughed and rolled her eyes. "Yeah, that's what I said about Sean and now I'm getting prepped for my wedding."

"Girl, shouldn't we be talking about just that and not my *not* date with Lachlan?"

"If I talk about my wedding, I'll just get nervous."

That surprised me. Katie was the definition of cool when it came to anything involving her upcoming nuptials. Things were planned to the minute and she was actually on schedule. "What, why?"

"I don't know. I mean I desperately want to be married, and all the attention of the wedding is going to be fantastic, but I'm just nervous for everything else."

"You mean Scotland." It wasn't a question. I already knew what she was thinking because I felt it too.

"Yeah. I have this whole life back home. Like, my job was dumb and my parents are spending their early retirement living in an RV and driving around, so it's not like living in Jersey would mean I had anyone but you, really. But it's just... weird. Like I didn't go to Scotland to find a man, but I found a great one... but it means giving up my life in New Jersey and everything else."

"But it's worth it, isn't it?"

She smiled, making her mask slip a bit off her cheeks, making her look like an overly-happy swamp creature.

"Completely. Like I'm going to have this amazing life with this guy who checks all the boxes."

"Then don't be scared. You're going to love it here."

"It is pretty amazing, isn't it?"

"Yup, so you know I'm going to visit every chance I get just so I can vacation without hotel fees."

"Consider my guest room your permanent residence then."

"Is your stuff going to be at Sean's by the time you get back from Paris?"

"I hope so. All the boxes I shipped will probably come while we're away, but his dad is going to sign for them."

"Beats going back to the job you hate in an apartment you pay way too much for."

"Why do you stay?"

"In Jersey?"

"No, your job."

I shrugged. "It's good money. I didn't want to stick though law school and take on all those loans, but I wasn't about to end up in a doublewide trailer like my parents. Being able to pay the bills is top priority."

She looked down at the raspberries that swirled in her champagne glass. "You know, you could just stay here for a bit longer... like forever and just find what makes you happy here."

"Yeah, I'll just quit my job, ship all my stuff, and crash on Lachlan's couch for a few years."

"Or in his bed."

THE SMALL CLOCK on the dresser showed one o'clock and I had already been dressed and made up, ready to go to lunch for half an hour. The day was still a bit chilly, so I wore a pair of white jeans with ripped knees, my black flats that I brought for nights out, and a dark red shirt that dipped down with a low V-neck and hung off one shoulder. It was reminiscent of the dress Lachlan first met me in and I hoped he liked it. Then I put in my diamond stud earrings, shoved gold bangles on my arm, and dabbed just a hint of Burberry's latest scent behind my ears and the top of my breasts.

When he knocked on my door, I made him wait a minute. I ran a brush through my gently waved hair again, which was curled just enough to give volume, but natural enough that it looked as if I might just wake up with hereditarily perfect locks. Then I took a final peek in the mirror before slowly opening the door.

"Ye look very nice," he said as I stepped out into the hallway. Unfortunately, he wasn't in a kilt. "Ye will no' need the bag though." He nodded down at my purse.

"Um… okay?"

"Bring it if ye like, but it's better to ride with as little as possible."

"Ride? Ride what?"

He gave me a funny look and said, "A horse."

"A horse?" I had ridden ponies at state fairs, but I was far from some kind of accomplished rider that was about to go galloping over the Scottish hillside like some historical romance heroine.

"Scared, are we?"

I scowled at him and tossed my purse on my bed before slamming the door shut. "As if. Lead the way, stable boy."

He laughed and took my hand. It was a little cliché, but our fingers fit well together and I liked walking down through the castle with him. He pointed out different portraits as we went, showing me his eighth uncle, great-great-great grandmother, and other ancestors who sat in puffy clothes, looking rather dazed and holding things like birds and riding crops in unnatural positions.

The cloudy, grey sky appeared to be lightening and the clouds disappearing as we stepped outside. We rounded the castle, the opposite way one would take to go to the gardens. But people milled around, planting additional bushels of flowers and hanging more string lights in the hedges.

"Hey, did they fix the garden lights for the wedding?" I asked.

The last thing Katie needed was to worry about bushes.

"Turns out that there was no' anythin' wrong. Someone decided it would be a fine idea to turn off the lights."

I had a stinking suspicion Katie was behind it, but I couldn't really be mad at her. As much as I wanted Lachlan to bend me over a birdbath or something the night before, I would have regretted doing the dirty out in public like that. One never knew who might have been watching.

The stables were small, tucked at the edge of the tree line, but clean and modern, obviously an addition that was much newer than the castle around it. Six stalls sat on either side and our footsteps echoed on the immaculate, polished floor. It was so spotless, I wouldn't know it housed a dozen horses if I didn't hear them stomping their hooves as we passed or snorting in excitement. They were beautiful beasts, but I was a little intimidated. They were a hell of a lot bigger than the docile ponies at the petting zoos.

He stopped us before a stall that was already open. A large black horse stood there, no saddle on his back, being bridled by a teenage boy. I unconsciously stepped back a pace when the animal dipped his massive head towards me to give my hair a good-natured sniff.

Lachlan smiled and pulled me close to him. "He's a good horse, my Hamish. He will no' hurt ye."

"I never said he would. But... but you don't expect me to ride him, right?" I asked, looking around to see if I could spy a reliable pony of a more manageable size.

"No' alone, in any case." He released my hand and beckoned the horse forward. In a smooth motion, he climbed aboard his back and looked at me expectantly.

"What?" I asked, my hands on my hips. I couldn't see what a horse had to do with lunch. Were we going to gallop along to an old-timey saloon? I just wanted some food and a method of transportation that wouldn't involve me snapping my neck.

He nodded down to my left, where the teenager was down on one knee, his fingers laced into a basket. "Step in with your left. He'll hoist ye up."

"Oh." I looked down at the boy, who didn't seem at all annoyed at having to lift up some American lady who was apparently afraid of horses. "Sorry, thank you." I took Lachlan's hand and stepped up with my left as instructed, apologizing to the actual stable boy the entire time. Before I knew it, I was sitting behind him, stiff as a board.

"Dear Lord."

"Ye'll live, lass. Just hold me tight about the middle and try no' to faint, aye?"

I nodded and flung my arms around his waist. In romance novels and on history drama shows, it always looks so romantic. The broad-shouldered Scot and his little lassie on horseback, smoothly traveling through mountainous terrain while their hair flowed behind them like a Pantene commercial. But in reality, it isn't all that bosom heaving. I was ten feet off the ground, on top of an animal that could turn on me at any moment, and had to rely on another person to keep me on or I could fall off and die.

As the horse began walking out of the stable, my arms involuntarily compressed around Lachlan like a vice.

"Relax, Rose," Lachlan said in a voice I assumed he

might also use for skittish horses. "I've been ridin' since I was wee. Perhaps even before I could walk, myself."

"Sounds like bad parenting."

He chuckled at my lame attempt at humor. "Maybe. But my point still stands. I will no' let ye fall to your death. Might ye bide a ride at a quicker pace?"

"Sure?"

His legs moved in front of mine a bit and the horse began a light—jog? Canter? Speed walk?—out towards the trees. I felt less steady than ever with nothing to keep my feet from flopping against the horse's sides. I tightened my legs against its flanks and pressed my cheek against Lachlan's back, my eyes shut tightly. My grip on him helped me from bouncing around too much and I tried to focus on something other than the hard ground passing beneath me.

I kept my mind on Lachlan, which I was stunned was actually harder than I expected. It seemed like the threat of death was really putting a damper on my libido. But the firm muscles beneath my palms *did* make the whole ordeal a little easier. It was almost possible to ignore the trees passing by us at a rapid pace.

After what seemed like an eternity, the horse stopped and I dared to open my eyes. It took a moment for them to adjust to the sunlight, but then I saw we were in a raised clearing beside a small, clear pond. The main tower of the castle was visible above the trees beyond and the only sounds I could hear were the light chirping of birds.

Lachlan dismounted and then helped me down, his hands firm on my hips. He looked down at me, the corners of his lips twitching, like he was trying not to laugh. "Will ye live, then?"

"No thanks to you," I said primly, patting at my wind-blown hair. "The view is great though."

"Would ye like lunch?"

"Oh, no. Back on the horse already?"

He laughed then and pushed the horse over a bit to a shaded spot where it began to eat grass happily. But with the animal moved away, I saw where Lachlan intended us to spend lunch. A large, plaid blanket was spread upon the ground, and a traditional wicker basket sat to one side.

"A picnic?" I asked.

"Aye. I thought ye might... I thought ye might like it." He brushed his hand through his hair and shifted from foot to foot. He looked hopeful, his lips set and his brows slightly raised as he waited for me to say something. "If ye'd rather go into town, then we can—"

"No, it's perfect."

He visibly relaxed. "Good. I didn't know what ye'd like, so I brought a bit o' everythin'."

Lachlan took my hand and placed me on the picnic blanket. I sat with my legs out to the side, in what I hoped would be an attractive pose. I wasn't used to sitting on the ground, avoided it even. But having a handsome Scottish guy take me on a surprise picnic in the countryside was making me a fan of roughing it... well, not *roughing it*, I guess, unless sleeping in a castle and having a perfectly packed meal served to me by a Scottish lord counted.

He sat down across from me and began unpacking the basket. It was one of those fancy kinds, one might think of rich people in the Hamptons using on their jaunts, with the plates and cutlery strapped to the inside of the lid. He took out two plates and freshly pressed linen napkins, then a bottle of red wine, which had been carefully wrapped.

"Nineteen seventy *Gaja Sorì Tildìn* suitable?" he asked, showing me the black bottle with its label displayed.

I shrugged. The last wine I had drunk at home came from a box, so I wasn't in a position to really judge anything. So I helpfully held out the glasses as he unscrewed it and poured out two generous doses. Then he unpacked the food. There were cold chicken sandwiches on freshly baked rolls, a spinach salad, chopped up fruits, some kind of potato dish, and a plate of pasties. I saw some other things wrapped up within that looked like little teacakes.

We ate in silence for a few moments, both avoiding each other's eyes. It was like I was back in high school or something where everything was new and neither one of us could think of something to say.

"Everything's delicious," I said, finally getting around to the wine. I had been dying to try it since I saw the black seal on the bottle that meant it was probably fancier than the kind I usually bought. But I didn't want to look like a total lush.

"I'm glad ye think so. And the wine?"

I took a sip but didn't experience any of the magic that I thought would follow an exclusive brand. It was good, but not life changing. "It's nice."

"Just nice?"

"It's *very* nice?" I tried.

"Maybe I should have packed up a bottle of tequila instead?"

"Maybe."

"So, I suppose this is the part we learn a wee bit about each other, aye?"

"What do you want to know?"

He pursed his lips, in what seemed to be his thinking mode. "Let's start with the basics. Job, pets, siblings, allergies, blood type?"

"Paralegal for a divorce attorney, no pets, no siblings, allergic to ragweed, and AB positive. You?"

"Well, I'm the esteemed laird o' this grand domain," he said with all seriousness, waving his arm in an arc. "I keep horses, sheep, chickens, there are ducks about, if ye count those. No siblings, bees, and O. Do ye like Scotland so far?"

"Love it. I always liked history, but never really had the chance to pursue it outside of it just being a hobby. Back home, I like to do a lot of reading and genealogy charts, learn about old architecture, but I couldn't do anything with that."

"Why not?"

I took another sip of wine and watched as he began unpacking the desserts. "My parents never really had money. I put myself through school and got a few certifications... I guess I didn't know if I could make real money with a history degree outside of being a teacher and I love kids... but not enough to think I'd ever be good at teaching them."

"What would ye want to do, if there were no limits?"

"That's tough. I know what I would do here. I'd travel around and see all those old chapels and graveyards, and do some research on things older than my home state."

"Aye, there's more history in Scotland than anywhere else I could picture. We had the Celts, the Vikings, the Romans, the Picts, the Christians... we were a right meltin' pot before America took the name on."

"I'd love to learn more. But I guess even though I'm out of time, Katie can send me books to add to my collection and I can do some good reading and try to make a list of things I want to see when I come back."

"Then, in the meantime, do ye care for some real Scottish dessert?" he asked, putting his glass down in the grass beside the blanket. "I can't say it's historically accurate, but it's from a Highland kitchen, which is just as well."

I leaned back a bit and relinquished my empty glass to the safety of the basket. I wanted dessert all right, but wasn't much in the mood for teacakes and scones. Biting my lip, I leaned forward slightly and pushed away the final plate of dessert. Several cakes rolled off and onto the blanket.

"Ye do no' want it?"

"I want something else more," I said, grabbing him by the shirt collar. He quickly lost balance, landing on top of me. And since I'm not a particularly strong woman, I think it was safe to say that he fell on purpose.

He had me pinned beneath him on the blanket, his knees between my legs and his body braced on his elbows. "We'll save the cake for later then, aye?"

I answered him with a kiss. Then we were off in a flurry of hands and lips. His fingers slipped beneath the hem of my shirt, teasing the revealed skin of my stomach and mine ran from his hair and over his shoulders to the buttons of his light grey oxford. But apparently I was too slow, because in one fluid motion, he pushed himself up and tore the shirt from his body, scattering the loose buttons across the plaid blanket.

Then his mouth was back where it belonged. His lips seared a path down to my neck as his hand slipped up my stomach and over the lacy cup of my bra. I inhaled sharply as he found a nipple and I ran my fingers over the smooth skin of his back. I cursed myself for being so shitfaced the first night we slept together when I could have been enjoying his body for the last few days in some sort of plaid-tinted sex haze.

I had just reached down to his belt buckle when the heavens opened up and rained down upon us… literally. A sudden downpour splashed us with an icy spray that killed the fire that had burned between us in an instant. I was too shocked to immediately move, but Lachlan did at once, rising rapidly to his feet and pulling me up with him.

"We should go back," he said as a strong wind whipped through the clearing, chilling me to the bone.

I looked up at the black sky above us, filled with traitorous cock-blocking clouds. "What the hell is this?"

He whistled to his horse, which trotted at once over to us. "This, my American Rose, is Scotland."

"What about the basket?" I asked as he lifted himself atop his mount.

"Leave it," he said, reaching out his hand for me to take, looking every bit the shirtless Highlander. "Someone will see it back to the kitchens."

He swung me behind him fairly easily, which probably sounded like the smooth motion one might imagine from a romance novel. But in reality, I had to half crawl myself into a sitting position before we started the ride back to the castle. I had my cheek pressed against his back, protecting me from the worst of the pelting rain.

For some reason, the trip back was a lot more pleasant, if one could ignore the stinging raindrops. Maybe it was the wine, or the short, charming lunch, but it was more likely the fact that I *did* feel a little like the heroine in a romance novel. I was charging through the Scottish Highlands in the rain, clinging to the muscular, shirtless back of a lord who set me on fire and was about to, hopefully, ravage me in a castle.

But more than that, I wanted to spend a little more time with him in a dryer setting. Without the ruined kilt or the awkwardness of our hen party night sitting between us like an impenetrable barrier, I found it very easy to just be with him. Beyond the physical, he was a good guy, easy to talk to, and I thought I couldn't have found a better shirtless Scot to picnic with.

A man came out from the castle and took the horse's reins as we both dismounted to the ground. We scurried inside, our hands clasped together, and brushed past the maid who was dusting a suit of armor beside the landing. We were both soaked and I felt sorry for whoever would have to clean up the trail of water we left in our wake. But any thought of that was soon cast aside when Lachlan stopped me not before my own bedroom door, but one closer to the mouth of the hall.

"Ye look cold," he said, his hand resting lightly on the knob. "I have blankets in my room, as well as a fireplace."

I wasn't all that cold, really. My rushing blood kept me more than comfortable, but I knew an opening when I saw one. "Good idea. Can't have us getting sick before the wedding. Katie would never forgive me."

His room was similar to mine, but much bigger and more personal. Tucked between the classic wood furniture, there were traces of modernity—a flat-screen TV on the wall, a framed sports jersey above a dresser, and a row of fancy watches on the nightstand.

I stood in the center of the room as he went to a wardrobe, pulling out a blanket and tucking it around my shoulders. Then he crossed to a large fireplace that looked just as old as a lot of the rest of the castle. A pair of stone lions held up a mantel and the Calder crest was etched above it. In seconds, he had lit a flame that crackled healthily in contrast to the sharp spattering of rain on the paned-glass windows.

"A real fire," I muttered, a little surprised.

"Your clothes are soaked through," he said quietly to me as he stepped closer.

I nodded. "A lot of rain outside."

"Ye'll catch your death, ye know."

"That's an old wives' tale. But I'd hate to make a puddle on the floor. It might warp the wood, and I can tell it's original."

"Very good o' ye to worry so about the architectural integrity o' my home."

He was close enough that I could reach out and touch him, and he was probably thinking the same thing. I dropped the blanket to the floor and kicked off my shoes. My heart was pounding in my chest and I pulled my wet shirt over my head, dropping it to the floor. It was then I realized how damp my skin was, as the cold air sent a chill down my spine. But I was also thankful for my choice of waterproof eye makeup so I didn't look completely like a drowned raccoon.

I expected Lachlan to make a move, but he was frozen, staring at me with his bright green eyes, his lips slightly parted. So I continued on with the show, taking my time to unbutton my skintight jeans, my gaze trained on his. Unfortunately, taking them off wasn't a graceful and seductive shimmy, but an act of peeling, struggling, and I had to yank them over my feet in a violent matter. Anyone ever put on skinny jeans right out of the shower? It was basically like that, only backwards and even less appealing than the sultry moves I was aiming for.

But then I was finally standing there in my carefully selected matching bra and panties. And then it was like a switch flipped suddenly, and Lachlan charged to me, slamming his lips onto mine. If our frantic motions had a soundtrack, "I Believe in a Thing Called Love" by The Darkness would be blaring.

I was finally able to unhook his belt and I slid it out of the loops in his pants, throwing it behind me. Then my fingers found the button and he helped me to unhook them, our mouths never leaving one another's. I could feel him beneath his Calvin Klein boxers and it took the lightest brush of my fingertips before he flung me atop his bed and rid himself of everything but his briefs.

"I've been waitin' for this," he growled, standing over me beside the bed. His hands ran down my sides and over my stomach, leaving a trail of gooseflesh in his wake. He teased the hem of my panties and I lifted my hips to allow him to pull them off, but he didn't. "No' so fast."

He hovered over me, nipping at the sensitive skin on my neck. His bare body against mine felt right and I arched my back, relishing the feel of my lace-covered breasts against his chest. He was all muscle, trim and athletic, and he was no stranger to a woman's body. He even rid me of my bra with one twist of his nimble fingers.

I moaned when he palmed my naked breast, but he silenced me with another deep kiss, our tongues entwining. The other hand glided down below, dipping beneath the lace. He slowly slipped a finger inside me, teasing me as he circled the delicate folds. But I was too ready to feel every bit of him and I pushed up, yanking down his briefs. My need was mirrored in his eyes and he reached into his nightstand, producing a condom.

I slid my underwear the rest of the way down as he sheathed himself and climbed on top of me. He only needed one thrust to be inside me and I gasped aloud at the sheer feeling of being so completely filled. He looked down at me, his gaze hooded with lust and my breath caught in my throat at zaps of electricity sparking to life within me.

When he started moving, I clawed at his hips, feeling so overwhelmed. His breath was hot against my neck and I craved more with each plunge. I wrapped my legs around his waist, giving him deeper purchase to my core and he groaned with the new angle afforded to him. He looked down at body as I writhed beneath him.

"Lord, you're so beautiful," he murmured, his thrusts growing quicker.

The familiar, orgasmic sensation was building within me and I cried out as he lifted the curve of my ass upwards. I had a fantastic view of his sculpted shoulders as I clung to him and when he reached down to grind his thumb against my clit, I came undone. The waves of release roared through my body and he had also found his own by the string of guttural Gaelic he growled into my hair.

He fell down beside me on his back and we both lay there, trying to catch our breaths in the aftereffects of some of the best sex I'd ever had. I felt completely drained and could barely muster the strength to open my eyes. But when I did, Lachlan was standing at the foot of his bed, naked as a jaybird... whatever that means. I didn't even feel him move.

"That was amazing," I said. "I can't believe we hadn't done that before."

"We did," he reminded me, climbing back beside me on the bed. "And if ye'd like, I would no' refuse ye another tumble in the sheets."

"Like you even had to ask."

I STRETCHED, CATLIKE, basking in the afterglow and fire-light, and Lachlan grinned down at me from his place beside the bed. His briefs were back on after round two, but I didn't feel strong enough to worry about such things as clothes and modesty. I let him look at my body, which was completely on display, but I didn't feel self-conscious at all. The way he looked at me with such appreciation made me feel almost powerful.

"I like when ye do that."

"Do what?" I asked, my arms leisurely draped above my head. I was tempted to tell him to 'paint me like one of his French girls' but didn't want to be weird.

"That." He nodded down at me and brushed a hand over the swell of my breast.

I batted his fingers away playfully. "No, not yet. I need some food and some electrolytes before we can do this all again. I could murder a burger right now."

"That's good, since dinner will be served in a few minutes."

"Up here?" I asked hopefully.

I needed to eat, but I didn't want to do it clothed and sitting at a table. I had finally gotten Lachlan naked and wasn't in a hurry to see him with a shirt on. It would be a goddamn shame.

But he shook his head and crossed to his dresser, taking a T-shirt out from one of the drawers and passing it to me. "Our absence will be noticed, as there's only the four o' us here."

I sat up and pulled the dove-grey shirt over my head. It

was soft against my skin and only added to my feeling of sleepiness. "Oh, it'll be fine. Can't we just stay here?" I attempted a sensual pout, but it was apparently a lot less persuasive than I hoped, because he didn't immediate jump my bones.

"As much as I would like nothin' more than to get back into bed with ye, we really should eat something."

"But then we'd have to put on pants."

"Sadly, that's true." He began picking up our discarded clothes and frowned. "It's all soaked through."

I shrugged and slid from the bed. The floor was cold beneath my feet. "It's okay. I'll just make a run for my room."

"I'll have all this washed for ye." He dropped everything in a pile in the corner. "Should we go down together, do ye think?"

"I don't think it warrants a conversation, honestly. I'll just come back here when I'm done. Wish I had time to shower first, though."

He smirked and slapped my ass. "We'll shower later."

I rolled my eyes and opened his bedroom door, looking out into the empty hallway before making a run for my room. It felt stark and bare compared to Lachlan's. But if I had my way, we'd be spending a lot more time in his bed during the rest of my time in Scotland.

When I went into the bathroom to freshen up, I was horrified. My once perfectly styled hair was what could only be described as "extreme bed head" and my waterproof makeup was a little smeared beneath my eyes. I even saw some teeth marks on my neck. My only saving grace was that Lachlan was clean-shaven, so I didn't have any beard burn, which was nice since I had sensitive skin.

I ran a brush hastily through my hair and wrapped it into a long braid over my shoulder. Then I just took off all my makeup before putting on some leggings and a sweater. I didn't really care if I was supposed to have been dressed for dinner. I just wanted to be cozy. Without Lachlan's body heat, it felt a lot chillier in the castle and I hoped dinner would be nice and quick so I could get back into his arms and between his sheets.

He was standing in the hallway when I came out, dressed casually in jeans and a plain black shirt. "All set?"

"Yep. Let's get in and out, fast."

"Don't worry, we'll make a quick meal out o' it. I want to get you back in my room in time for dessert." He had whispered the words into my hair and it sent a shiver of anticipation down my spine.

Katie and Sean were already sitting at the table when we entered, picking over the remains of the salad on their plates. It had been casually set for four, with each place close together on one end. Lachlan and I sat on the same side of the table and I tried very hard to look normal, but Katie's sly grin told me she knew what was going on. Still, the manners of the Scottish were apparently wearing off on her, because all she did was smile and welcome us.

I began eating my salad, knowing the next course wouldn't be done until the lord of the manner had finished his first. Sean carried on most of the conversation, talking about how the rain would brighten the greenery in the garden and that their families would be arriving soon, and a few other things that I probably should have been listening to. But it wasn't my fault that I couldn't pay attention. Lachlan had placed his hand upon my knee as soon as we sat down to eat.

"Did you two have a nice lunch?" Katie asked politely as soon as there was a lull in the wedding conversation.

"Aye, it was very nice," Lachlan replied. "We went up to the hills by the loch."

I thought it would be awkward if I didn't say anything, so I added, "Until we got rained out."

"Oh, did you get wet, Rosie Posey?" Katie's tone was even and she didn't even crack a smile.

Heat burned my cheeks and neck. I didn't dare look at her and pondered some kind of escape plan. Luckily, the next course finally arrived in a bustle of trays and fresh wine. Then Lachlan saved the day by saying something about how great the lamb looked, which drove the conversation to wool production or something.

As one course followed another, his hand, which had first settled on my knee, had begun to inch up my thigh. His fingers made lazy circles that I could feel distinctly through the thin fabric of my leggings. By the time a light dessert of cake and berries was served… well, if I were wearing a skirt, we would have been halfway to third base.

"You okay, Rosie?" Katie asked in a singsong voice that grated on my nerves. "You've hardly even touched your cake."

"Totally fine, just filled up on dinner, I guess."

"Oh, maybe the four of us should play a board game after dinner? Maybe something that can take a while. Lachlan, do you have Monopoly? I'm a little rusty on the rules, but I'm sure I can reread the instructions quick enough."

I glared at her and attempted to kick her under the table, but the stupid thing was too big to make contact. My toes only touched air. So she ignored me and looked pleasantly over at Lachlan, the corners of her lips twitching.

Lachlan glanced at me. "Ach, no, I do no' think so."

"Isn't there?" Sean asked, apparently innocent of Katie's ridiculousness and looked to be ardently concerned about some railroad real estate.

Lachlan shook his head. "No, don't think so."

"I could have sworn it—"

"No," Lachlan said a bit more firmly. "I'm… quite tired and wish to turn in early. I have a few business things to tend to before turnin' in."

"I bet you do," Katie mumbled into her wine.

"Me too," I announced. "This jet lag is lasting forever."

"Shall I escort ye upstairs, Rose?" Lachlan asked.

I nodded with another dirty look in Katie's direction and

followed Lachlan from the room at a leisurely pace. But as soon as we were out of sight of the dining room, we clasped hands and ran through the halls, up the stairs, and into Lachlan's room. We were probably loud in the empty halls of the castle, but when one was about to bed the hottest guy in the Highlands, she really didn't care about the volume.

As soon as the door closed, we began undressing each other in a flurry of roaming hands and mouths. And when I was once again stripped down to my underwear, Lachlan backed away and turned to go into the bathroom. I hadn't really had a chance to admire the view from behind, and I couldn't find anything to complain about. It was like he had been carved out of marble.

"Comin' to join me?" he asked playfully as he slipped his briefs off and left them on the floor in the doorway.

I nodded and thanked scientists the world over for birth control pills. We had quietly and quickly discussed the cleanliness of our personal health, a bit belatedly after our first time, and it was nice to not have to worry about condoms and pausing the moment when a Scottish lord was inviting you to join him in the shower.

His bathroom was larger than mine, more lavish by far, and he had already had the water running when I stepped in. He stood beside the opening to the shower, which was the size of a small walk-in closet, watching me hungrily. I took my time unhooking my bra and shimmying out of my panties, which was a lot smoother than when I had to fight my way out of my soaked jeans.

The water was hot and as soon as the glass door was shut, we were enveloped in a cloud of steam that fogged the glass. I slipped my arms around his waist and he immediately kissed me, his hands sliding smoothly down my wet back. He hardened against my stomach and I smiled against his lips. He let out a small moan when I wrapped my fingers around his member and began moving up and down.

His hands travelled freely over my breasts, cupping my ass, teasing my slit as the water cascaded over us. And then he suddenly turned me around, pressing me against the cool marble of the shower wall. I arched my back invitingly and he ran his fingers down my spine. I let out a sharp gasp as he roughly grabbed my ass.

I could feel him, hard as a rock behind me. I wanted him—badly—and glanced at him over my shoulder. "I want you inside me."

That was all it took. He was in me in a moment, hard and hot, thrusting as one hand dug into my thigh, the other holding both of my hands over my head like I was getting the hottest pat down of my life. My cheek was pressed against the marble as he drove in to me. This was shower sex like I had never had before. It was rough and dirty and I liked it more than I probably should. But who was I kidding? It was what I came to Scotland intending to do and Lachlan did it well.

Chapter Eight

I HAD LEFT Lachlan's room the next morning when the castle was still quiet. We were scheduled to go on some sort of scenic boat ride and I wanted to get myself together enough that it didn't look like I was going right from his bed. I'm sure Katie wouldn't let me live it down if I did.

Once I was in my room, I thought about what someone would wear on a boat in Scotland. I had been warned to dress warmly, but how warm was that? A sweater? A parka? A light spring jacket in the season's newest pastel? I decided to go down to Katie's room and figure it out.

She was just coming down the hall when I opened my bedroom door, a heavy bag in her hands. Her eyes were wide and it almost seemed like she was shocked to see me. "Hey!"

"Hey yourself," I said, letting her inside. "I was just coming to find you."

"I figured you'd be my way sooner or later to get something out of my closet."

"Well, it's not like you told me we would be out on some freezing cold adventures before I came here."

She shrugged and dumped her load onto my perfectly

made bed. "It's probably not going to be that cold. But just in case, it's a good thing you can fit into most of my stuff. And we didn't really have this planned until it was clear you and Lachlan were... whatever you are now."

"So because we're getting along, we're being dragged out to sea?"

"It's supposed to be really cool. We're just going to take a little ride up and down the coast."

I sifted through the pile of thick sweaters and coats. "Is it going to really be this cold out there?"

"It's smarter to layer up, just in case so if it's warm, you can just strip a bit."

I pulled a charcoal-colored sweater from the pile and a black jacket. "Will this be okay?"

"It's why I brought it."

I thought she would leave, but instead she sat on the edge of my bed, looking at me.

"What?"

"So... how are things?"

"Fine? Why are you being so weird?"

"Because your bed hasn't been slept in and you're wearing last night's outfit."

My cheeks burned for a moment and I busied myself with packing up the rest of her things. "You're being ridiculous."

"You know, you could do worse than a Scottish laird."

"Again, you're being ridiculous."

"Shh, just let it happen." She fell back against my pillows and yawned. "Anyways, how is it?"

"How's what?"

"Things between you two. Come on, Rose, spill. Are you in love yet? Going to run off together?"

"We're just having fun, Katie."

"Nonstop fun by the look of your hair."

I patted my head self-consciously, feeling the tangles. "Shut up. Is Sorcha coming?"

"No, she has to work."

I don't know why, but that surprised me. I didn't imagine Sorcha even having a job. "Where does she work?"

"She's a painter, actually. She does those murals in people's homes for, like, nurseries and stuff while waiting for her actual canvas pieces to start to sell. She does a lot of art shows as well."

I pictured her in a studio, her high cheekbones splattered with paint, wearing a little French beret. It suited her. "So how are the three of them related?"

"Their dads are all brothers. Sean's dad ended up being a barrister, Lachlan's dad married his mom who was the lady of the Calder clan and they did the estate stuff, and then Sorcha's dad works in breweries I think."

"Oh, that's pretty cool. So, when are we leaving?"

"About an hour. It'll be a bit of a car ride to the boat. They're serving a light breakfast downstairs, but we'll be eating lunch on the water."

"Wait," I said as she stood up and readied herself to leave. "Don't you get seasick?"

"Yep. But Sean picked me up some stuff from the pharmacy that he swears will help."

"For your sake, I hope it does."

AFTER I PUT my makeup on and braided my hair down my back, I put my borrowed sweater on over a T-shirt, and then added a pair of leggings and my boots. When I went downstairs to the dining room, the three of them were already at the table. They were picking at plates of eggs, sausages, and buns. While I wouldn't classify it as a light breakfast, I was still ready to fill my plate.

"Good morning," I said as I sat down beside Lachlan, across from Katie.

"Good mornin'," Lachlan greeted with a small smile. His hand immediately fell upon my leg, settling there with a reassuring weight. "I fixed ye some coffee. Did ye sleep well?"

I took the mug, still hot, and breathed in the aroma before taking a sip. It was sweet and just how I took it. I wondered how he knew and my heart squeezed with the gesture. "Thanks for the coffee, and I did. I guess you can say your friendly neighborhood ghost has been taking good care of me."

Sean set his teacup back on the saucer with more force

than necessary. "Come off it, you two. Everyone knows Rose didn't sleep in her own bed last night. Might as well end the façade."

"Yeah," Kate agreed. "Lachlan knows *exactly* how Rose slept."

Already over being the butt of their jokes, I cut in. "Okay, so what's the deal with this boat thing?"

Lachlan put down his fork and leaned back in his chair. "We'll just be takin' a sailboat down the coast o' the harbor towards the North Sea. The water should be fairly calm and there's a good chance we'll see some dolphin."

"So we're going dolphin watching?"

"I thought we'd perhaps take it over to that coastal castle." He looked at Sean. "What do ye think, fancy showin' the lasses MacMillian ruins?"

That got my full attention. An ancient castle was way cooler than some random pod of dolphins I could see at home. "Will we be able to see it from the boat?"

"We'll take a small one up to the shore, aye?"

Sean pushed up the sleeve of his shirt and glanced at his watch. "We should leave now. The car should be ready."

I pushed away my half-eaten breakfast, a gasp getting caught in my throat, along with a piece of a roll I was eating, when I saw what Lachlan was wearing. He had on a thick, cream sweater, brown boots, and to my extreme delight, a dark red-and-green kilt. While I thought something like that would be a little chilly out in the open water, who was I to tell a Scotsman how to wear a kilt?

I must have been staring because Lachlan placed a hand on my shoulder and whispered, "Are ye well, lass?"

"What?" I looked around and saw we were the only people left in the dining room.

"I asked if you're alright. Ye've no' blinked in a few minutes."

Averting my eyes, I stood and shrugged on my jacket. "Sorry, I was thinking about something."

"Oh, were you?" he asked, a glint in his eye. "Come on with ye then, Rose. They'll be waitin' for us."

He looped an arm around my shoulder and led me from the dining room. I could feel the course fabric of his kilt against my knuckles and part of me wanted to play sick and take Lachlan with me. I could see some fish and rocks anytime I wanted, but there was a time limit on tartan.

When we stepped out into the bright sunlight, Lachlan bent down and said into my ear, "I know what you're thinkin' and I promise there'll be more than enough time later."

With that, he opened the front passenger side door for me, then took his place behind the wheel. Katie and Sean were cuddled up in the back, looking at something on her phone that was related to his cigar bar. It was apparently a point of contention between them because they bickered over the pros and cons of having everyone stomping around the castle grounds with cigars in in their mouths like 1920s mobsters.

Katie and I had already been to coastal Nairn, where I had gotten a number of fun little souvenirs. The day we had gone, the weather was lovely, and although it was sunny out now, it could very well be much colder out in the water. But at least it didn't look much like it was going to rain, making it a rare day in the Highlands.

Lachlan parked in a narrow lot overlooking the water. He was first out of the car and was opening my door before I even had a chance to unbuckle my seat belt. When I had two feet on the pavement, he took my hand and interlaced my fingers with his, causing me to have to shoot an ecstatic Katie a dirty look to stop her from teasing. But still, I liked the small display of affection. It came so naturally with Lachlan.

The lines of boats on the docks ranged from little row-boats to ones with massive, looming masts. We strode down one long dock, with Lachlan and Sean randomly saying hello to people as we passed them in a familiar manner. It looked like they came to the harbor fairly frequently and when we got to the last slip, I saw why.

"Here she is!" Sean announced, waving to a sleek, white-and-blue sailboat.

It was one of the larger docked in the harbor, clearly sporting both a large cabin, raised captain's station, and a small dinghy fastened to the back. When I thought about sailboats, they were much, much, *much* smaller in my mind. In contrast, this one conjured images in my head of top international human rights lawyer Amal Clooney and her husband George on a tropical vacation. All that was missing was the sun, sand, and unflattering paparazzi shots.

"Yay, the *Bonny Bàta*!" Katie said.

"What?" I asked, wondering what in the world a *bàta* was.

"It's Lachlan and Sean's family boat. It was being repainted and refurbished forever, so I've never gotten to go on it."

I looked at Lachlan with wide eyes. "This is *your* boat?"

"It's a Mackinnon boat," he said, pulling me along to the stairs. "If ye'd like to get technical, it belongs officially to Sorcha's father for the most part, but he's out at his whisky brewery presently."

"Whisky brewery?"

"Aye, it's a small one. More of a hobby, really."

I narrowed my eyes at him when I saw the corners of his lip twitch. "Okay, so I feel like you're lying and his little *hobby* is less of a hobby and more of a large company. Am I right?"

"Perhaps a wee bit. Ye might have heard o' *Bearded Bard's Whisky*?"

Katie caught on to our conversation. "Hold up. You guys never told me Sorcha's dad is the *Bearded Bard Whisky* guy! We drank that all the time in college."

"I think I actually have some in my liquor cabinet at home," I whispered, wondering how many of my drunken nights were somehow related to Sorcha. In fact, learning that she was apparently some kind of whisky heiress made a lot of sense. Girl could handle her alcohol. "It's a shame she couldn't come."

"She's no' one for open water."

"Neither is Katie."

She was already looking a little green around the gills and stuck her tongue out at me. "I took something, so I'm looking forward to a nice, little ride."

I shook my head and let Lachlan help me to the main deck. It was dark, shiny wood that was framed with gold and I could hardly feel the motion of the waves beneath. A man in a perfectly pressed white suit and trimmed beard strode meaningfully up to us, a serious look on his face.

"Morning, sirs," he said with a nod at both Sean and Lachlan. "And to you, ladies."

Katie gave me a sideways glance at being addressed so formally, and the moment the man turned to speak to Lachlan, she dipped a small curtsy in my direction. I stifled a laugh with a series of fake coughs, causing Lachlan to look my way in concern.

"Don't tell me ye have no stomach for water either, Rose?" he asked, patting me on the back.

I swallowed the last of my giggles and said, "Me? Love the ocean. I was basically raised on Jet Skis and shrimp cocktail like any other self-respecting Jersey girl."

To his credit, he didn't even do a double take. "Very

well. Katie, Rose, this is Captain Fergus and he'll be takin' us out today."

"Look at the *Gorton's* fisherman over there," Katie muttered to me as the captain scratched his grey beard, looking over some little notebook with a crewmember. "Where's his pipe?"

"He probably only saves it for special occasions."

"Stop your chatting and come have a seat up here," Sean called down at us. He and Lachlan were peering at us from over a railing above.

I led the way up a few small steps to a raised platform that sat just below the captain's station. It was a decadent lounge area with built-in loveseats, chairs, and couches. They were all set into the deck with a low table in the center. It was all beneath the... mast? Sails? The big stick where the bottom of the sail puffs out. It was well above our heads, even when standing, and cast a very long shadow upon the dock.

"Fancy a life vest, love?" Sean asked as Katie clung close to him on one of the couches.

She shot him a dirty look. "I can swim, I just get motion sickness."

"This boat is great," I said to Lachlan as Katie and Sean went back and forth about if seasickness bracelets or pills were more effective.

"Aye, we've spent a lot o' time on this ship since we were wee bairns. When it's warmer, this part below us opens up for a Jacuzzi."

I looked down, seeing nothing but more polished wood under my boots. "The floor?"

"The seats come up, the table slides away, and the pool fills up."

"Wow." By the castle, title, and apparent lack of need for a career, Lachlan had money, but something about a hot tub on a boat really drove it home. He, Sean, and apparently Sorcha, had all grown up in something most of us only read about in magazines. "Wait, if you and Sean were so close growing up, why is your accent so much more... Scottish?"

He smiled and drew me closer as the lines were cast off and we began to slowly motor out of the marina. "Well, we did no' grow up in the castle together, he's more o' a city lad. We both had private educations, but I spent more time in the country durin' our off seasons while he later finished his schooling in London. Is it that obvious?"

"Sorta. He still has that accent but yours is really strong."

"I hope that's a compliment," he said with a wry smile.

"The very best kind. It goes with the kilt." I traced one red line in the tartan with my fingertip, finishing the trail high on his thigh.

Suddenly, the boat jerked a bit and Katie let out a small shriek as the sail dropped suddenly above us. We rapidly began cruising out of the harbor, leaving clusters of small fishing boats and colorful, waterfront houses in our wake. I was glad I braided my hair and put on a jacket, as the wind was cool against my cheeks.

"Aren't your legs cold?" I asked Lachlan, looking at the bare swatch of knee between where his boots ended and the kilt began.

He looked at me like I had just said something completely ridiculous. "Cold? Why would I be cold?"

I rolled my eyes, assuming that Scottish men were made of different stuff. "Never mind."

A young woman in the same white uniform as the captain appeared beside our chairs, holding a tray with four large mugs on it. "Somethin' warm for ye?" Without waiting for a response, she handed each of us a steaming, fragrant mug.

I lifted mine to my lips, tasting honey whisky and something else I couldn't identify. It was like a hug in a mug, warming me from the tips of my toes to the top of my head the instant I took my first sip. While the weather wasn't terribly frigid, the drink helped me to feel completely relaxed and allowed me to really enjoy the view from behind my cat-eye shades.

The coastline of Nairn was picturesque. Houses dotted the shoreline past the large city that overtook the land up the marina. The water was a dark blue, interspersed with small, white-tipped waves, but the sailboat cut through them like a hot knife through butter. But at the speed we were traveling, Nairn was soon disappearing, allowing for high cliffs and hills to be visible on the land we were skimming.

The woman shortly returned with the first course for

lunch and glasses of white wine. I hadn't realized we had already been out in the water for more than two hours, but a glance at Lachlan's Rolex told me we had. So we dined first on a summer salad of greens, walnuts, and light raspberry vinaigrette. Then came fresh salmon over rice and a dessert of some kind of tart. By the time the dishes were cleared. I was feeling like life on a sailboat wouldn't be that bad.

After about another hour of more hot, honeyed whisky, light conversation, and a vomit-free Katie, Lachlan put an arm around my shoulders and dropped his lips to my ear so I could hear him over the rush of water. "Do ye see those stones?" He pointed to the shore on our right, where tucked beneath two large outcroppings, sat something that looked like a dilapidated pile of rocks.

"Yes, why?"

"That's where we're headed. It was once the keep of the MacMillian family. While they were no' a clan, the family was rich and powerful, enough so that they could have such a grand spot."

"It doesn't look like much. Your ruined castle is much more impressive."

"Trust me, ye will no' be disappointed when we see it up close."

Katie stood and passed her glass to Sean. "Come down the bathroom with me, Rose?"

"Sure." I untangled myself from Lachlan's arm and drained the last of my whisky. "Do you know where it is?"

"In the cabin, right?" she guessed, looking down at Sean.

When he nodded, we carefully rounded the edge of the railing towards the stairs we had first come up. While the crew had begun to pull down the sails, slowing the boat significantly, it still rocked a bit. I kept my hand on the rails until Katie opened a door that revealed a short staircase.

The cabin within gave only a small peek into what else we couldn't see. Perfectly shined wood covered every surface of the elaborate living room, which held fancy green, leather furniture and a fully stocked bar. A flat-screen TV was even nestled between two tall bookcases. The shelves had little bars over them, which held the books into place. If I couldn't see water out the little porthole windows, I wouldn't even know I was in a boat.

"Wow..." Katie trailed her finger over the top of the bar. "This is so nice."

"It is. Did you know Sean... did you know he came from money? Like *real* money when you guys met?"

She shook her head, still looking around. "Not at all. He had a regular house and at first, we basically just stayed in my hotel rooms. Even when we went on dates and he paid, I thought he was just showing off to impress me, you know? It wasn't until after we got engaged that I really even met his family and found out all this."

"How are we even going to find the bathroom? This is way bigger than I thought."

"Just try doors, I guess." She opened the first, which held

a hallway. "Come on."

WHEN WE CAME up to the top deck, the *Gorton's* fisherman announced that the small boat was ready to take us to shore. The black dinghy on the back of the boat was already in the water, being held close to the hull by a crewman.

"You want me to get in that?" Katie asked with an accusatory look at the dinghy.

Sean gave her a little squeeze and said, "Don't fret. We'll be on shore in a moment."

"Yeah, come on, Katie. It's just like being on a Jet Ski, and I know you like those." I was already in the dinghy, sitting near Lachlan who had a hand on the little outboard motor.

"You said you could swim," Sean reminded her with a gentle push.

"Ugh. I'll get in the stupid, little boat," she grumbled. "But if I die without getting married, I expect you guys to drag my dead body down the aisle and make it legal. I won't have my headstone say *Daughter, Sister, Friend,* Almost *Wife.*"

Despite her brave façade, she looked more ready to vomit than I would have expected. As her friend, I felt bad for her. But as her best friend, I just had to laugh. She had Sean's hand in a death grip and was staring over at the cliffs with wide eyes like we were going to drop her off on the rocky shore of some desert island and leave her to die. To his credit, Sean just held her tight.

Lachlan, in contrast, looked completely at ease as we glided towards the thin strip of beach. The salt water sprayed over us as we bumped along the breaking waves. As the ruins came closer into view, I saw that it did resemble some sort of large manor house after all, but without the roof. It was surrounded by a low, stone wall and was set high between the cliffs.

When the bottom of the dinghy brushed against the rocky beach, Lachlan cut the engine and hopped into the shin-high water. It was good he had on such high boots, since the ocean had to be freezing. However, I did enjoy the visual of Lachlan single-handedly pulling the dingy further onto the beach.

"Come on," he said, holding his hands out to me. I was about to take one, but he shook his head. "No, put your hands on my shoulders. I'll take ye to dry land."

I did what he asked and he gracefully picked me up, swinging me over to the beach. The sand sank under my feet, but my boots stayed dry. Sean tried to do the same for Katie, but he ended up almost dropping her when a wave came and hooked him below the knees.

"See?" Lachlan whispered to me as he took up the rope again and brought the dinghy further up on the pebbles. "City boy and country lad. He may have a more polished accent, but who's the real winner here?"

"Ugh, that was terrible," Katie groaned, staggering up the beach until she hit a spot of dry sand. "I feel like death."

"Shall we stay here for a wee bit, then?" Sean suggested. "We'll sit down and take some deep breaths."

She nodded and plopped down on the ground, her eyes closed and her head between her knees.

"Come on, I'll give ye the tour." Lachlan took my hand and began leading me up to the fence.

"What about them?"

"Sean's a big lad. He can fend for himself... and Kathryn too, for that matter."

We hiked up the slope, the ground becoming easier to manage the closer to the house we came. On either side of us were sheer cliffs, looming over, looking ready to topple over onto us. The stone wall was almost perfectly intact, three feet high and boasting no gates. We had to climb over it to see the rest of what was left of the house.

It was made of the same rock as the walls, two stories high, with those little slit windows one saw in history books. There was something surrounding it that gave it a different feel than Lachlan's ruined castle-turned-restaurant. It felt more like when someone would take the first few steps into a graveyard and the hairs on the back of their neck stood up. Like we weren't supposed to be there and it was letting us know we weren't entirely welcome.

"This place was built about the same time my residence

was," he explained as I craned my neck to take it all in.

"But why is it falling down? Doesn't anyone care about it?"

"Things changed after the Jacobite Rebellion. Whatever clans did no' bend to the English had to pay the price. My family managed to keep what they had while others were no' so lucky. Besides, it's pricey keepin' up house in a castle."

"I bet. I balk at my power bill in the winter sometimes and I live in a one-bedroom apartment."

"It's part o' the reason I refurbished the castle. I'll be openin' it to the public soon, for events and the like. I don't want to lose the history o' my clan, nor let the castle to end up like this."

"That's really smart."

He looked at me and smiled. "Ye think so?"

"Completely." I walked to where the door used to be, my hands brushing over the time worn rock. "Tell me more about the house."

"Well, it was built in the middle ages, partially carved out o' these cliffs. That's why it's survived all these years while others have crumbled around it."

He poked his head inside first and peered around for a moment, then motioned for me to follow. Inside, light poured in freely, due to half the roof being piled on the ground in the center of the entrance. The space below our feet was mostly tufts of grass with the rest being made up of broken and crushed stones. I heard the call of seabirds and it echoed in the long-forgotten hold.

"Is it safe here?" I asked, looking at a staircase that led upwards.

"Aye. Everythin' that could fall already has, for the most part, and I know where else is no' safe."

Our hands intertwined, we walked deeper into the ruins. The farther we went down the narrow corridors, the quieter it became and soon I couldn't even hear the roar of the ocean. I ran my hand over the damp walls as we explored, looking into room after empty room. We saw the old kitchen, which held a massive fireplace, the chimney long since gone, and a pile of animal bones sat discarded in a corner.

"This is really cool," I said, looking out one of the many little windows after brushing aside a creeping vine.

"Wait until ye see the upstairs."

"Can we go up there? It's safe?"

"Safe enough, come on."

Since the stone staircase didn't have a railing, I pressed myself flush to the walls as I crept up in front of Lachlan. He looked much more at ease in the precarious climb, watching more of what I was doing instead of his own footing. To say I was relieved to get back to solid ground was an understatement and I felt much better, if I ignored the fact that parts of the roof had already collapsed at some point.

"Here's where the family would sleep," Lachlan said, motioning to one of the many empty doorframes. "This is the largest and most coveted since it was above the kitchens."

"Why would that be best?"

"The heat from that massive kitchen would keep ye very warm without needin' to have your own fire burnin'."

I followed him again, seeing many more little rooms that probably once held children and other family members. While it had been more than a century since anyone had even attempted to live there, it almost felt like trespassing into someone's home. It was strange how places like that still held life, hundreds of years since the last inhabitants had moved on.

"This is my favorite place in the castle," Lachlan said with a smile as we stepped into the final room on the floor.

The face of the far wall, along with part of the ceiling, was long gone, leaving the room partially open to the ocean below. Salty winds blew lightly in, making a whistling noise as they carried on through the rest of the house. The beach we came in on was far below us and Katie and Sean had left the dinghy and were somewhere else. The sailboat was still anchored out in the water and I had a better view of the Scottish landscape.

Placing both hands on what was left of the wall, I leaned forward to get a better look to either side of me. Lachlan came up behind me, enveloping me in his arms. I closed my eyes and leaned back against him. He felt so solid and real, maybe even more so than the ancient keep we stood in.

But even more real than the stone beneath my fingers or

his chest against my back were my growing feelings. Things hadn't felt so easy and true for a long time. Everything with Lachlan was effortless and natural. It was a sharp contrast to the dating scene at home where I felt like I needed to keep up. With Lachlan, I could happily go along for the off-road ride. He never seemed to want me to be anything other than what I was and it made me think of what Katie had said about how she knew Sean was the one.

"Do ye like it?" Lachlan asked, tilting his head down to bring his lips to my neck.

"I do."

Chapter Nine

T HE NEXT MORNING I awoke to the sounds of car doors and small shrieks of joy. I buried my head deeper into the pillows... but it wasn't the bedding I was curled up against, it was Lachlan's chest. Eyes still closed with sleep, he clutched me tighter to him as if out of impulse. It was a lovely place to lie, in all honesty. I relaxed in his arms, ready to fall asleep again, when there was a loud knock on the door.

"No, thank you," Lachlan grumbled into my hair.

There was another series of knocks.

"What the bleedin' hell is it?" he roared, jarring me to sharp attention.

I rubbed my eyes, my heart beating frantically in alarm.

"Our mums are here." It was Sean. He sounded like he was laughing and I swore I heard Katie giggling as well.

"Alright," Lachlan called back.

"Shall I bring yours up?" he asked through the door. "You know she hasn't seen the place since your renovations and I'm sure she'll love to see the bedrooms."

"Fuck off, ye wee pest, and keep my mum out o' this!"

Two loud laughs answered him and two sets of footsteps retreated back down the hall.

"Ach, now we have to get up." He moaned, holding me closer.

"I'm so tired."

"How do ye think *I* feel? *You* are the one who kept me up all night."

"I didn't hear any complaining."

"And ye never will," he promised, pushing himself up and stretching. I loved the way his muscles responded with the movements, giving me different angles to appreciate as he twisted and turned. "We can't put it off anymore."

"What time is it?"

"Almost noon."

I slowly sat up and slid off the bed. "Um… do you know where my clothes are?"

"A wee bit here, some there."

"Helpful."

Avoiding his gaze, I stepped around the room, gathering my discarded clothes. I wasn't shy exactly, but there was something a little different about collecting my pants and shimmying into them for the walk of shame back to my room. Well, I wasn't really sure if it was technically a walk of shame if no one was there to witness it.

"So… Rose… I had a nice… lunch with ye the other day and it's a shame it got rained out, and yesterday we ate with Sean and Kathryn," he said, handing me my sweater. "Maybe ye'd like to have dinner together tonight, just the two o' us?"

"We're already going to have dinner together. All the guests are arriving now."

He frowned slightly, which only somewhat marred the view, since he was still only in his briefs. "Aye... a full house. I'd almost forgotten."

"What a terrible host you are," I chastised, running my hand down his chest, over the black lines of the family crest tattoo.

His green eyes sparkled. "Don't commit to somethin' ye can no' finish, lass."

I tugged a bit on the waistband of his boxers and grinned, letting it snap into place. "Still, I'll see you for dinner, and for lunch, and for everything else until the wedding's over."

"So three whole days?" He kissed me on the cheek and slapped my ass. "Off with ye, now."

I slipped out of his room and went into mine, feeling frustrated and more than a little wound up. But much to my surprise, Katie was sitting on my bed, looking fresh as a daisy in a white sundress. A white, wide-brimmed fascinator sat at an angle on her hair. Upon closer inspection, a bunch of feathers and flowers were tucked to one side along with a birdcage veil.

"Good day, you little hussy!"

I sighed as I opened my wardrobe and flipped through

my clothes. "Is it warm out?"

"Very. We're having the welcome lunch outside, remember? So dress cute. Anyways, this whole thing with you and Lachlan is all amazing and worked out way better than I planned. I feel like one of those matchmakers on TV."

"Katie, relax. I'm not planning a quickie wedding or anything," I said, stripping out of my clothes to redress in a pink number that was classy in design, but showed enough cleavage that I hoped I could use to lure Lachlan upstairs before dinner again. Then I went into the bathroom to wash my face and sort out my mussed mane.

Katie followed, dragging the small chair that sat beside the bed. When my face was washed, she made me sit while I put on my makeup and she began brushing my hair out. She was always a fan of playing with my hair and she was pretty good at hiding any walk of shame dos that any of our sorority sisters came back to the house with.

"Lachlan is a good guy, you know," she said as she began braiding.

"I know."

"I mean he's really smart and loves kids. And he's allergic to bees, but has no hereditary markers that would be passed down to his children, making him prime breeding stock."

I put down my mascara and looked at her in the mirror. "Katie, why are you so obsessed with me and Lachlan? What's really going on?"

"Why am I obsessed with my best friend in the whole

world getting together with my future husband's cousin? Well, I don't know, Rose, why would the idea of that thrill me?" She ran the brush she held roughly through my hair, tugging it hard.

"Ouch! Come on, Katie. What's going on?"

She pursed her lips for a moment then heaved a sigh, putting the brush down. "If you and Lachlan fall in love then you'll come live in Scotland and we can be neighbors and live together forever and raise our kids together and go shopping on the weekends and have holidays and—"

I turned around and put my hand on hers. "You knew that I was always going to go home after the wedding. I have to. I have my job and my apartment, real responsibilities that I need to take care of."

"It doesn't mean I have to like it. I mean, you don't like your job, your apartment will be way too quiet without me sleeping over all the time, and aren't you just so sick and tired of being responsible?"

Her words hit me in the gut. I was tired of being that person, the one who took care of everything, wore blacks and greys to a desk job where I was treated like an unpaid intern, despite my college degree. I wanted passion and fun and the kind of interesting things I had only seen in Scotland. I had a taste of who I could be and I didn't want to let it go, even though I had to.

"And I'll come all the time, whenever you want me to."

"I know." She pouted and turned me back to the mirror,

finishing up the double braids that wound around to the back of my head. The rest fell in thick, smooth waves. "And if you want, I'll stop meddling and just enjoy you being here while you are. Now, we're late and really need to get down to the welcome lunch."

"Nice hat, by the way," I told her, tapping one of the fake, white flowers, trying to ignore the pit in my stomach.

"Don't be jealous," she sang, going back over by the bed to a bag I hadn't noticed before. "I got you one, too!"

It was the same size and style as hers, but in a crème color. The brim was gauzy and held up a few silk peonies. I'm not particularly a hat person, but I let Katie pin it to my hair and it was actually a flattering look. I could see why the Kate Middletons and Queen Letizias of the world wore them all the time.

I applied a nude lipstick that complemented the earthy tones of my eye makeup and slipped on my wedge sandals. I pulled on my usual bangles and added diamond stud earrings, and then followed Katie out of the room. We passed Lachlan's door, but I didn't hear anything inside. It was foolish to think he would still be hanging out in his bedroom when he was lord and host for the wedding weekend.

The garden was full of people. Women in sundresses, men in kilts and slacks, and children in their Sunday best milled around the hedges and picked at the light lunch that was spread under a white tent and served by staff in crisp suits. A small band was set up off to one side and was playing a merry little number that had some couples slow dancing in the grass. As soon as we stepped on the lawn, a man with a tray offered us champagne.

I scanned the crowd, instinctively looking for Lachlan. He stood beside the tent, looking rather dashing in his kilt and jacket. I was immediately flooded with the desire to drag him back up to his room. We had technically had sex for the first time with him wrapped up in plaid, but really, it hardly even counted and I was much more interested in banging him when he was clean shaven and dressed like the proper lord he was.

"Down, girl," Katie muttered, yanking me in the opposite direction of where Lachlan was. "Keep it in your pants for a little bit. There are some other minor nobles here, so we need to be on our best behavior."

"Do I need to curtsy?" I didn't actually know how to curtsy, and wished I thought to practice a bit, just in case.

She stopped walking for a moment, her brows knit, and then shrugged and continued on. "Honestly, I didn't think to ask Sean. So… probably not since we're both American and I don't think there are like kings and queens here, so I wouldn't worry about it."

"Sounds like a plan."

In turn, I was introduced to a knight, two dukes, a lord, three ladies, and a duchess with a rather loud lap dog that snapped and snarled at me as I passed. Since I wasn't really secure in my curtsying ability, I did a little bobbing motion that was halfway between a bow and a knee bend when I thought I should. Now, not everyone had some fancy title, but I met more blue bloods than I ever thought I would in an hour span.

Neither Katie nor I were very much at ease, but at least she knew some of the parties in attendance and did what she could to play the charming hostess. Although, next to the demure ladies, she seemed to stick out, but not in a bad way to me. She was like a wildflower in a sea of roses, a little less classic, but beautiful and untamed. Again, I thought to how weird my life would be without her vibrant energy cutting up the monotony of my days.

When we finally came around to Sean, I excused myself, leaving the two lovebirds to continue the rounds. I was making a beeline for the bar when Lachlan caught my eye. He was talking to some older man, who was dressed similarly in a kilt, although in a different color. I thought I would leave him to chat, but he motioned for me to join him and I could almost feel his gaze raking down my body as I grew near.

"Rose." He greeted me politely, then leaned down as if he were politely kissing my cheek and whispered, "I can no' wait to get ye out o' that dress."

I swallowed, feeling something stir within me that I didn't want to leave. "Hello, Lachlan."

"Rose, this is Dougal MacDonnell," he told me. "Dougal, this is the maid of honor, Rose Hensel."

"How do ye do?" Dougal asked politely in perfectly rounded Scots.

"I'm very well, thank you. And yourself?"

His grey brows rose and he grinned. "Ach, an American! How do ye find Scotland?"

"It's a beautiful country and I've greatly enjoyed my visit. My only regret is that I won't get the chance to further explore."

Dougal nodded. "Aye, ours is a country rich in history. Now, do excuse me. I must find my wife."

"Any relation?" I asked Lachlan once Dougal was gone.

"No, he's just a business acquaintance."

"In what way?"

"I think I told ye I wanted to open the castle a bit? Well, he's overseen some o' the larger renovations to the stonework in the castle. His company is very good at keepin' things as true to history as possible so the parts that have been redone are a wee less noticeable."

"That sounds like a very interesting job."

"I suppose ye'd think so, with your interests."

"Hey, people like me are the ones who are going to want to come see this place. Don't knock your demographic." I looked back around at the guests. "I bet some of these people even live in their own castles, so it's not like you could pitch your history to them."

"Ach, no. Only three o' them live in the older estates so perhaps a few will darken my doors for a look. He took a step backwards, taking me with him into the garden maze and out of the direct view of the guests. Then he brushed some of my loose hair over my shoulder, his fingers lingering on the bare skin below my cap sleeve. "Ye look very beautiful today, Rose."

The way Lachlan said my name still sent a shiver down my spine. I had always had an ordinary name, but it sounded sensual and dirty coming out of his mouth. My middle clenched with the sudden memory of him saying my name the night before. "And you look very handsome in your kilt."

"Does that mean ye might take me into your chambers later to see what's beneath it?" he asked playfully, encasing my waist with his hands.

"No. I want you to keep it on."

He grinned and was about to reply when someone called his name from outside the hedges. He frowned. "Duty calls."

With a small kiss on the lips, he left me there to catch my breath in the privacy of the maze. I could hardly wait for the day to be over so we could escape upstairs to his bedroom. It was only just after one in the afternoon and the thought of it being another nine or ten hours until we could be together was almost too much to handle. But it was more than lust that made me crave him. I just wanted to be in his company, to sit and talk and learn about him and listen to him talk about his plans for the castle, since that seemed to make his face light up.

When I felt sorted enough to be seen by the general public, I made sure my tiny, British hat was still firmly attached and stepped back into the lawn. I planned on getting another glass of champagne and maybe finding Katie if she wasn't too busy doing bridal things. And if she was, I hoped I would find Sorcha somewhere in the crowd. If anyone could get my mind off of Lachlan, it would be her.

I was walking through the guests to the tent when I saw her, a blonde goddess that checked all the boxes in what someone would think when the word *goddess* came up. Tall and tan, her perfectly highlighted blonde hair was wrapped in a chignon and the pale pink dress she wore made mine look cheap in comparison. There was also a dove-grey Birkin bag looped over the crook of her arm that matched her own fancy, little hat and I'd bet my collection of knockoff Louis Vuittons it was the real thing.

Miss Legs glided through the crowd, obviously feeling at home and familiar with everyone. With the blonde hair and model looks, I assumed she was a cousin and thanked my lucky red, white, and blue stars I wasn't up against her for a job or something. With the poise and class she oozed, she probably had me beat in the brains category as well.

The second glass of chilled champagne was just what I needed and I came upon Sorcha as I turned away from the tent. She was looking flashy in an electric-blue dress, but I noted that she was hatless.

"Aren't you just a lovely rose, Rose?" she said, kissing me on both cheeks. "I haven't seen you since the hen night.

How is everything?"

"Good! I've been at the castle the past two nights to help with last-minute things. You know how weddings can be." I debated telling her about Lachlan, but what girl would really want to hear about who her cousin was banging?

"Brilliant of you, truly. I'm so glad Katie and Sean are keeping things intimate."

I looked around at the assembled guests. There were probably around eighty people, more than Katie had first said. "This is intimate?"

"Anything less than a hundred is cozy for us! Have you met everyone?"

"Nearly. There are a few people though and—"

Sorcha groaned loudly. "Why is *she* here?"

"Who?"

"Lady Fenella of Slutsville, that cow."

My brows rose at the disgust in Sorcha's voice. She seemed so positive all the time and it was strange to hear her speak with such venom. "What?"

"*Her.*" She pointed towards the gardens behind me and I turned.

Miss Legs, or Lady Fenella apparently, was draped over Lachlan's chest. She had one hand on his arm and was nestling into his neck in a way that told me they hadn't just met. While he wasn't exactly cuddling back, he didn't go out of his way to untangle himself either. It made an angry heat bubble up inside me, filling my cheeks with hot rage.

"What. The. Fuck?"

"I know. She waltzes in here whenever she pleases and Lachlan follows her about like some neglected pet. It's absolutely horrid, but no one ever says anything because her daddy owns all these draft breweries and blah, blah, blah. One time—" She stopped suddenly and looked at me, bewilderment on her face. "What is it?"

"Nothing."

"You look as if someone's just shat on your shoes."

"It's nothing." I downed my champagne, still looking at Lachlan and Fenella, who were speaking, their heads close together.

Sorcha's eyes darted from me to them and back again. "Oh, Lord. I've said something out of line."

"No, you didn't." I fought to keep my voice steady and appear as if I was above it all, but bitter tears of embarrassment and hurt pricked my lids. I felt cheap and stupid. Sure, I wasn't expecting a proposal and a happily ever after with Lachlan, but being replaced so swiftly after we were just planning another night together felt awful.

"I didn't know that you and he—"

"Are nothing."

"I'm sorry... I didn't know that anything..."

"Please, don't worry. I'm just... I'm just going to go to the restroom."

I turned on my heel and hurried back towards the castle. I had no right to cry at one of Katie's wedding events, or at all, really. While I was beginning to feel more for Lachlan than I had the right to admit, we were still nothing more than a pair of people having a good time. Though, to me, it was still a slight betrayal of what I thought we shared. Seeing him with another girl stung like a slap to the face.

I went to the nearest bathroom beside the pavilion and looked at myself in the mirror. My makeup was fully intact, down to the lipstick I had applied just an hour before. But my eyes were glassy and if I blinked, the tears would fall over. So I took a bit of tissue and dabbed at my eyes until I was sure I wasn't in danger of any scenes.

Then the door opened and someone said, "Oh, pardon me, I didn't know anyone was in here." Then they turned to leave the room.

"No, don't worry. It's my fault for not locking the door. I'm finished."

Lady Legs—Fenella—turned back into the restroom, a pleasant smile on her flawless face. "Thank you ever so much."

I nodded in return and scurried out. She was so beautiful, noble, and polite to strangers. I wanted to hate her, but it wasn't fair. She hadn't done anything to me and I had no right to hold her past, present, or future relationship with Lachlan against her. He wasn't my boyfriend. He wasn't my anything.

I felt a bit better when I stepped back outside, until I saw Lachlan striding towards me, looking rather concerned. I hated how gorgeous he looked in the bright afternoon sun, which lit his hair with a golden glow and bounced off his bronze skin.

"Rose, are ye well?" he asked, his hand resting gently on my shoulder. "I saw ye run inside."

I shrugged him off and scanned the crowd for a familiar face to save me, which was stupid since I only knew a handful of people. "I'm fine."

"Ye do no' look fine."

"What a lovely compliment."

He grimaced. "I didn't mean it like that, Rose. Ye look lovely, as always. But your expression is… are ye cross with me?"

"Whatever gave you that idea?" My heart began to pound in my ears and I wanted desperately for someone to come to my aid and give me a reason to run.

Thankfully someone did, just not a someone I would have personally chosen.

"Darling," Fenella cooed, laying her long fingers on Lachlan's arm. "Daddy wished to speak with you about breeding that black gelding you fancy so much." She seemed to notice me standing there and said, "Oh, hello again."

I forced a smile. "Hi."

Lachlan cleared his throat. "Fenella, this is Rose Hensel, the maid o' honor. Rose, this is Lady Fenella MacGinnian."

"Charmed to meet you." Fenella's voice had a perfect accented clip to it and I found it grating. The feeling got worse when she moved closer to Lachlan and pressed against him. "Now, darling, can you spare a moment to speak with Daddy?"

Lachlan turned to me. "I saw Katie and Sorcha by the far gate. Ye remember how to get there, aye?"

My cheeks were beginning to hurt with the smile I was forcing. "Of course. Lovely to meet you, Lady MacGinnian."

"Please, call me Lady Fenella."

The walk to the far gate was literal. It felt like it took forever to steer through the guests and around the hedges. And when I finally did find Sorcha and Katie, whispering together and looking more than a little concerned, I wondered if it had been a bad move to go searching for them in the first place.

"Oh, Rose!" Katie's face was sorrowful and she pulled me into a light hug, which didn't really help in the "not crying" department. "Sorcha's just told me what happened and I'm just so mad for you. She's an idiot, and I know I don't actually know her, but apparently she's a cow."

"Nothing happened," I said firmly, more to myself than them.

Sorcha patted me on the shoulder. "Fenella's old news. She's only here because whatever rich sod she was shagging probably smartened up and left her."

"Whatever Lachlan does isn't any of my business. Now, shouldn't we be socializing or something?" I was eager to get back into the crowd where they could have a distraction from pitying me.

They exchanged worried glances, then nodded, silently following me back to the party. I wanted another glass of champagne, but figured it was probably better to skip the alcohol when I was feeling that shitty. Nothing good would come of me getting wasted. I'd probably end up sobbing all over Lachlan and threatening to throw Lady Legs into the fountain.

Luckily, I found something else to occupy my mind. A tall, dark-blond man stood talking to Katie's mom, but I didn't recognize him from her side of the family. The addition of a kilt that matched Sean's firmly labeled him as a Scotsman. While I had already met a hot guy in a kilt, I had been severely burned. Now it was time to not only meet a guy who could pull off tartan, but one that was actually nice. The best way to get over a man would be under a new one. I just hoped it worked.

I elbowed Sorcha and asked, "Who's he?"

"That's our cousin Richard, another groomsman," she said once she had figured out who I was talking about. "He's our second cousin on the Mackinnon side. His da is my da's cousin."

Without waiting to hear more about their family tree, I straightened my back and walked over to Katie's mom. "Hello, Gloria!"

"Rosie, you look fantastic." She gave me one of her short, motherly squeezes. "Love this shade on you. I was just telling

Richard here that Katie has the prettiest bridesmaids."

"And I told her that one of those bridesmaids was my blood relation." Richard's tone was playful and he smiled warmly down at me before extending a hand. "Richard Mackinnon, the formerly absent groomsman."

"Rose Hensel, Katie's maid of honor." I didn't feel any special sparks when our fingers touched, or care very much when he pulled away like when Lachlan touched me. But Richard was still handsome enough to fill the void and make me forget.

"Will ye be stayin' at the castle?"

"Yes. I've been here since the day before yesterday. You?"

"Just for the night. I've only just gotten back from a business location this mornin' and I'm awaitin' all my things from Belgium, so I need to leave first thing after the weddin'." Then he looked to where Gloria had been standing. "It appears we've lost Kathryn's mother."

"It's fine. They have a lot of family in, so she probably has to welcome a lot of people."

"I'm sorry if this is out of line, but were ye at the hen's night?"

"Yes, I was. Were you also dressed as an extra from *Braveheart*?"

He sighed dramatically. "I'm afraid so. But it's all in good fun. I recall you were the purple one, aye?"

"Yes, I was." I was a little surprised he remembered who I was. Sure, there were only three of us in tutus that night, but it was nice to be remembered. Out of the corner of my eye, I saw Lachlan beside the band, twirling Lady Legs as they danced with the other couples.

Richard must have followed my gaze because he said, "Great couple, Lachlan and Fenella. Have ye been introduced to her yet?"

"Yes, I have," I said through my teeth. "Are they a couple?"

"I believe so. But I've been away on business for months and haven't had the occasion to catch up with my extended family. Besides, Lachlan is never normally very open about who he's seein'."

My heart painfully skipped a beat at the thought that Lachlan and Lady Legs might have actually been currently dating and Sorcha just didn't have a clue. It was possible I had been an accidental home wrecker. It made me sick to think about. I wasn't the kind of girl to sleep with taken men. I refused to be some dirty little secret.

"Would ye like to dance, Rose?" he asked with a smile. "I admit I have two left feet, but it is a weddin' celebration after all."

"I'd love to."

I took his proffered arm and allowed him to lead me to the makeshift dance floor, just in time for another slow song that had all the dancing couples spinning in leisurely circles. I tried my best to look like I was having fun toddling from side to side with some guy I had no interest in, mainly so

Lachlan wouldn't see the effect he had on me. So I attempted to keep an ongoing dialogue with Richard about Scotland, the weather, Belgium, and anything else that came to mind.

When we turned at a new angle, I saw Lachlan watching us, thunder on his face. So I leaned in closer to Richard, and rested my head upon his shoulder gently, as many of the other women did with their partners. Lachlan would get a taste of his own medicine. He was too far away to hear what innocent words we were speaking, but my body language was on point.

Then Lachlan was there, his jaw set tightly and Lady Legs abandoned off to the side with a martini in hand. "Richard, cousin, good to see ye. We were afraid we'd need someone else to stand up at the alter with us."

"There's the laird!" Richard came to a stop and unhanded me, clapping Lachlan on the back. "Kathryn's maid of honor and I were just getting' to know each other."

He turned to me. "Is that so?"

"Very," I replied sweetly.

He studied my face for a moment and then said, "Richard, I'm goin' to have to steal Rose from ye now. Official weddin' business."

And without waiting for Richard's response, he took my hand and pulled me away from the party. Then he kept walking until we were on the side of the castle that was hidden from the white tent and prying eyes. Anger at him began to boil again. My intention was to make him jealous, but I was also mad at him to dare to be jealous. It was all rather confusing.

Then he pressed me against the wall and kissed me hard. For a moment, my knees went weak and I welcomed his mouth on mine. But then I remembered Lady Legs and I pushed him away with both hands before righting my tousled fascinator. Any pain I felt emotionally was replaced with red-hot anger.

"What was that for?"

"What was *that* for?" He looked so confused, like what I did was the last thing he expected of me.

"Why did you just kiss me like that?"

"Because you're gorgeous in that color, ye looked fantastic naked in my bed today, and now your off chattin' with my prat o' a cousin."

"Richard's very nice, thank you." I crossed my arms, mainly to keep from touching him.

"Aye, he's so nice, he would never dare do this."

"Do wha—"

He silenced me with another kiss, this time with more need and primal urgency than before. My traitorous body melted in his arms again and I gave in to every kiss and caress he threw my way. I didn't even fight when his hand began lifting the hem of my dress and I felt the wool of his kilt against my bare thigh. Damn him, I wanted him, even though he was never even mine to begin with.

I wondered if he was going to raise my skirt right there and take me against the wall. I wouldn't have really complained any and found the added danger of getting caught made the entire ordeal even more arousing. I reached down to his kilt, trying to jerk it up, but he pulled away, panting slightly.

"What the hell was that?" I asked, coming to my senses like I had just been doused with cold water.

Fenella was there. He had no reason to start kissing me. And I had no reason to let him.

"Why were you all over my cousin like that?"

"I don't think it's any of your business!"

"It *is* my business when a lass wakes up in *my* bed and then no' even two hours later, is actin' like she's about to get into my own cousin's by nightfall!"

Smack!

I don't know what came over me in that moment, but I was deeply offended at the implication that I was going to sleep with Richard. My palm stung with the aftereffects of the slap and his cheek was reddening by the second. My own were also on fire, but not because he had hit me back, but because I was ashamed, embarrassed, and irritated with him. I had never raised my hand in anger, but it was an impulsive action that I couldn't take back.

His face softened and he said, "Rose, I did no' mean—"

I held up my hand, which was shaking slightly. "Don't, Lachlan. I'm a big believer that when someone shows you who they are, you should take them at their word. And you've told me who, or what, you think *I* am and I won't stand here for a second longer listening to some shit excuse about how you had a slip of the tongue. So-called slips of the tongue are always an indication of a person's real thoughts. So go back to your *girlfriend* and leave me the hell alone."

I spun around and hurried back to the relative safety of the party. But then I saw Lady Legs shooting daggers at me from her large, brown eyes. Seeing her made me feel worse and I could hardly blame her for hating me. I almost went to her, to tell her what had happened between Lachlan and me. But when she looked me up and down, judgment and scorn thick in her gaze, I turned on my heel and stalked towards Katie and Sorcha.

"Good, you're here." Katie pressed a champagne flute into my hands. "Hair and makeup start at one tomorrow afternoon in my rooms. But you can come early for snacks and drinks."

She was trying her best to act as if everything was normal for my sake and I loved her for it. "That sounds great."

"Rose!" Lachlan called out to me.

I glanced over my shoulder at him then turned to Sorcha and said, "I don't want to talk to him."

She nodded and yelled back, "Lachlan, Sean's looking for you."

"Sorcha, do no' go tellin' lies. I only wish to—"

"No. Go find Sean. There's a problem with the caterer."

"What caterer?" I heard him ask from behind me. "Everythin' is bein' made here at the castle."

"Go ask him about it. I'm just the messenger."

When he had gone, Katie visibly relaxed and reverted back into her no-nonsense bride persona. "Now that that's dealt with, let's talk hairstyles."

Chapter Ten

I WANTED TO ditch dinner altogether, but my absence would be noted, especially with so few people staying in the castle. It would be Katie's parents, her little brother Mason, her grandpa, Sean's parents, Sorcha, Richard, some other male cousin I didn't care enough to remember his name, and Lady Legs and her dad. The last thing I wanted to do was sit at a table with her and Lachlan, but I reminded myself it was all for Katie.

Dinner was going to be a bit on the fancy side in celebration of both families being together and I wanted to look good. Not just nice as I did before, but straight-up unforgettable. Sure, Lady Legs had a title, money, breeding, perfect skin, and probably literally shit glitter since it wasn't like I actually saw her eat any food, but I wanted to look better.

Everything Katie owned was at Sean's home in Edinburgh, but she had brought half her wardrobe to the castle to give her a wide selection based on the varied weather. So I basically had a whole boutique at my disposable. She was a bit thinner, taller, and leaner than I was, but I could fit into a fair amount of her things. And if my chest was a little more squished and prominent, who was I to complain?

With her fashion skills, nimble hair-dressing fingers, and constant reminders I was a beautiful fairy princess that deserved everything good in the world, I ended up looking just how I pictured. I had taken one of her pale purple wrap dresses that showed ample cleavage without being too obscene. There was a fine lace overlay and the scalloped hem that hit just above my knees. Paired with some strappy gold shoes and my hair being twisted up into a casually messy pile atop my head, Katie declared me a masterpiece.

I had to admit that I felt a little better about everything. At least if I was pushed aside for some stunning heiress, it wasn't because I looked bad. But the closer we drew to the dining room, the more uncomfortable I felt. It wasn't like I had much of an appetite for the moment, so I wouldn't be able to even stomach the meal.

There were already guests in the dining room when we entered. Katie's parents and brother sat beside Sean on one side of the long table. She pulled me to the other side and I sat down beside her, wondering who would end up sitting in the empty space beside me. Turned out, it was Richard.

"Is this seat taken?"

I shook my head and tried to smile. As much as I loved a good flirt fest, I wasn't really in the mood. So I settled on being polite, but not overly friendly. "No, go ahead."

It was then Sorcha came down and I wished she had been a few seconds earlier so she could be beside me. Still, she sat across from Katie, next to Sean's parents. Fenella was the next to arrive, glittering in a skin-tight silver number that looked pretty out of place in the decadent, dark wood of the room. She looked around at us and sat at the table opposite Richard, careful to leave an empty space between her and Sorcha.

Sorcha caught my eye and pretended to vomit into her crystal goblet, which made me feel a bit better.

Then Lachlan strode in, still wearing his kilt and looking as handsome as ever. His green eyes tore down my body and I had to turn my head when fire reached my cheeks. There were two empty chairs at the table, one across from me and one at the other end, facing Katie's dad. Ultimately, he settled in a chair between Sorcha and Fenella, who immediately scooted a bit closer to him.

Katie squeezed my hand under the tablecloth and I smiled at her, trying to signal I was okay. Lachlan tried to catch my eye, but then the staff appeared with the first dish; a kind of soup that didn't taste right to me. As soon as we had all taken the first mouthful, Lady Legs decided it was time to be annoying.

"Lachlan, it's such a shame that Daddy needed to leave so suddenly," she said.

"Oh, aye."

"He says he'd still like to set up a meeting with you at his office."

"I'll keep it in mind."

She glanced my way for a split second, and then returned to stirring her soup and peering up at him with dramatic doe eyes. "Lachlan, do you remember when we went on safari two years ago?"

"Aye."

The rest of the table was still quiet, probably feeling the strained awkwardness that had fallen over our side. Sorcha was gagging quietly between mouthfuls, Katie and Sean were sharing nervous glances, Richard was listening politely, and I was stuck in the middle of it all.

"Where did ye safari?" Richard asked with a level of interest. "I've been to Zimbabwe, but it's been years."

Fenella's red lips curled into a smile at finally being prompted to tell the story she was obviously dying to share. "Well, Daddy had some business associates in Uganda and I said to Lachlan, why didn't we go with him for a little holiday? Lachlan was so busy with work, he barely had time for me." She pouted for emphasis before continuing. "And we stayed at this charming little estate in the thick of things. What was is called, Lachlan?"

"Ugandan Pride," he answered, pushing away his bowl and beckoning to the staff for the next course.

"And we stayed in these adorable little huts, do you remember, Lachlan?"

He nodded, still not looking at her.

She placed her hand on his arm. "And we hardly had the time to see *any* animals at all, did we, Lachlan? We were told there were ever so many, but never seemed to find the energy to leave our room."

He didn't respond, but looked up at me. I averted my eyes, not feeling up to taking another bite of dinner. Katie must have sensed my unease because she began loudly talking about how the weather was set to be fine for her wedding day. The topic carried us through two more courses and half the dessert, when Fenella opened her mouth to start talking again.

But Lachlan cut her off, midbreath, and stood quickly from his seat. He raised his wineglass and started, "It's been my pleasure to host the weddin' proceedin's these past few days and for the next that follow. It is my wish that Kathryn and Sean continue on the way to happiness and enjoy a long and prosperous marriage. *Slàinte*."

Everyone raised their glasses in return, calling out, "*Slàinte*."

I took that as the cue that we were allowed to leave and said a general good night to the table, saying that I needed my beauty sleep for next day. Sean's parents followed suit to their separate rooms and I was glad they did, so it didn't seem too weird that I left. Logically, there wasn't anything for me to feel jealous about, but I still felt a pang of unease with a hint of anger when I saw Lady Legs fawning over Lachlan. If anything, she had much more of a claim on him, seeing that they had a shared history... and perhaps a future as well.

When I got to my room, I locked the door before stripping out of my borrowed gown and washing off the carefully painted-on makeup I thought would have made me feel better—acting like a kind of armor against the jealousy that bubbled in my chest. I pulled out all the hairpins, stacking them neatly beside the sink, thinking about how it would be one of my last two nights in the castle. I thought I would be sad to leave, but with feeling so embarrassed at my replacement, I was more than excited to get on the plane home and get back to my predictable, painless life.

I changed into a tank top and shorts for bed, and then slipped beneath the covers. I opened up a book I had bought in the shops on my second day in Scotland. It was a collection of poems by Robert Burns. I was never one for poetry and had originally purchased it just as a souvenir of something very Scottish. But something about my wounded pride and hurt heart felt the need to crack the spine and read.

A while later when I was about to turn off my lamp and try to sleep, there was a knock on my door. It wasn't Katie, since she would have probably just tried to walk in or text me from her room, but I wasn't expecting anyone else. I was debating the need to actually get out of bed when the person spoke.

"Rose? It's me, Lachlan," he began through the wood. "I don't know if you're in there, but if ye are, I have somethin' to say."

He was met with silence because there was no way I was

responding to that.

"Aye, Fenella and I dated for a long time, but it's over now… been over for almost a year, or more. We were practically children when we first met and I thought she was who I wanted to be with… until I grew up."

I still said nothing.

"Christ, Rose, will ye no' speak to me?" He sounded sad, tortured even. It would be a lie to say it didn't please me a little to hear him so torn up. But I wasn't a cruel woman. Most of the time.

"I'm not interested, Lachlan," I called out.

"So ye *are* in there."

"Where the hell else would I be?"

"Will ye come out and speak to me?"

"Why should I?"

"Because I have the keys, lass, and I could come in if I wished, but I'd rather be a gentleman about it." There was a little jangle from out in the hallway.

I scowled at the door, but saw no other alternative than to open it. I placed my book on the bed, careful to keep my place and then crossed over the hardwood to the door. He stood there, still dressed as he was for dinner, holding a ring of old-fashioned keys in his hand and looking rather more hopeful than I thought he should.

"What do you want, Lachlan?"

"I want to speak with ye, Rose."

I crossed my arms over my chest and leaned against the

doorframe. I was trying to give off the *I don't give a fuck* vibe, but his piercing green eyes and kilt made it rather hard to focus on being stone cold.

When he didn't immediately start talking, I asked, "Are you going to say something, or just stare at me?"

"Mind if I do a bit o' both?" He shot me a cheeky grin, which fell when I rolled my eyes. "Fine, no jokes. I know what ye think o' Fenella and what everyone else does, too. But you're all wrong about everythin'."

"Then why is she here?"

"Her father's been in business with my father and my uncles for years. Our families go back probably longer than this castle's been standin' as it is now."

"So what's your point, *Lachlan*?"

"My bloody point, *Rose*, is that I did no' invite her and if I could do so without embarassin' the happy couple and myself, I'd toss her out now. Especially with ye bein' so cross with me over it." He took a step closer to me and I didn't move away. "Are ye cross with me, Rose?"

"Why ever would you think that?"

"I don't even like Fenella."

"Okay, so you don't like your ex. Who cares?"

"You, for one."

"I do not!" I hissed, trying to get my point across without waking up the other guests who had so recently taking up residence in the rooms between ours.

"Ye do, and that's fine. When I saw ye with Richard,

flirtin' with him so openly before me, I wanted to strap him."

"Is that why you pulled me behind a wall and basically called me a slut?"

He sighed and rubbed the back of his neck before continuing. "I'm sorry I said what I did, but I'm no' sorry I took ye away from him. He's no' right for ye, Rose."

"Right for me?" I snorted. "I'm only here for two more days. I'm not looking for Mr. Right or a proposal of love or a wedding in the fucking countryside, Lachlan. I have two days and nights left in Scotland and all I wanted to do was see my best friend get married and have a good time."

"Then have a good time with *me*, Rose." He reached up and cupped my cheek. "We're good together, you and I, and we'll have two good days and two great nights. I don't want Fenella or anyone else but *you*."

Between his words and the look of want he gave me, I had no choice but to bend to his will. He kissed me and I let him, the ring of keys clattering loudly to the wooden floor as he wrapped his arms around me. Being held by him felt better than I dared admit and I leaned into his lips. I would, however, admit that he was a damn good kisser.

But then he broke away, his hands still on my hips. "I need to attend to a few more things for the weddin' tomorrow. Can ye wait a bit while I sort it?"

"Do you need help?"

"No, it'll only take an hour or so."

"Then will you come back?"

"If ye want me to." It was an answer, but spoken more like a question.

I slipped a finger down his chest and brushed against the waistband of his plaid. "Wear the kilt and maybe I can be persuaded."

"Consider it done." He brushed another kiss against my lips and bent down, scooping up the key ring. He left me in the doorway and I closed it behind him, climbing back into bed to wait.

⟫⟫⟩⟨⟨⟨

A SLAMMING DOOR jarred me awake. The clock said it was almost one in the morning, three hours after I had told Lachlan to come back. He had said he wouldn't be long, but I thought three hours was more than sufficient. And I wondered if he had come and found me sleeping and thought it better to let me rest.

So, I slowly peeked out to the hallway, spotting a streak of light coming from under his door. I moved to step towards it when the door opened with a creak. But instead of seeing Lachlan, Fenella appeared, wrapped in a bath towel.

I must have gasped aloud because her head turned towards me and she grinned. "Oops. I've been spotted!" Then she scurried down the corridor and into another room that I assumed had been hers.

Lachlan was the next to make an appearance, his shirt untucked and top buttoned undone. I steeled myself and cleared my throat to announce my presence to the cozy midnight meeting.

He whipped in my direction and he blinked in surprise. "Rose," he started, taking a step towards me.

I held up my hand. "You know, I never really pinned you as a playboy. Sure, you know how to show a girl a good time, but I at least didn't think you'd be the sort to double dip. What was your plan? Send her back to her room when you were finished with her and then come to me for round two? Disgusting."

His mouth hung open and he shook his head. "No, ye do no' understand. I—"

"I might be young, an American, a foreigner that's unfamiliar with your cultured ways, but I'm not an idiot." My voice rose in volume, but I didn't conceal it. "So news flash, Lord Lachlan of wherever the fuck this is, you might think I've been blinded by the glitz and glamour of this castle and your title and a stupid picnic on a hill, but I haven't been. I see who you are. And I don't fucking like it."

It looked like he was going to say something else, but I turned on my heel and slammed my bedroom door, my heart hammering painfully in my chest. It was like I was going to be sick and cry and maybe even do both at the same time. At least the bathroom was nice.

There was a knock on my door and I knew it was him.

"Fuck off, Lachlan."

"Rose, please."

I slid down the door and to the floor, my back against the wood that moved slightly with each rapping of his knuckles. "Lachlan, please... fuck *off*."

"Rose," he began in a low voice. His mouth must have been almost directly against the door. "Rose, I know what it looked like, but I swear nothin' happened. She came and I sent her away."

I bit my lip, trying to force back the tears that threatened to fall. I had told him I wasn't some dumb American that he could fool, but that was exactly what had happened. I was swayed by an accented set of abs and head of blond hair. I fell for whatever game he wanted to play and came back for more, enjoying the attention. Sure, I had come to Scotland with the idea I'd sow my wild oats with a kilted man, but I never dreamed it would be so ridiculously painful when a casual fling ended.

If I could allow myself a bit of honesty, I would admit it hurt. It killed me to think he thought I was so disposable, although that was exactly how I had once thought of him. I was a hypocrite, an idiot, and so unprepared that I had become so emotionally attached to Lachlan. He was more than a hot guy in a kilt. He was smart, and witty, and knew how to make me laugh. But my attempt at a Highland fling had ended in tears, at least on my end, and I hated it.

"Rose, *m'eudail*, open the door, aye?" he pleaded, tearing

at my heartstrings. "I was lyin' earlier about havin' the keys to let myself in. Please, open the door?"

I waited in silence for several minutes until I heard the creaking of floorboards and the closing of a door. He was gone and in two days, I would be as well.

Chapter Eleven

I SLEPT VERY little, tossing and turning and regretting every moment I had spent with Lachlan. Well, maybe "regret" isn't the right term, but "grieved." The days and nights in his company had been more than amazing and I wanted to hold on to the feeling I had when I thought about his hand on my hip or his long stories of Scottish lore. But then again, how good could they have been if all it took was some ex whose daddy owned half of Scotland to bat her lashes for him to leave me in the dust?

My eyes were red and puffy and I lay in bed with a cold washcloth over them until it was almost ten in the morning. I texted Katie, asking if she was awake and if she needed me, then returned my compress. I didn't want my terrible night to result in terrible pictures for Katie.

My phone dinged and I slid open the screen.

Katie: *Moring Rosie Posey! IT'S MY WEDDING DAY!!!*

Me: *I know :) are you still in bed?*

Katie: *Obvi. Can't be seen until it's my turn to walk down the aisle!*

Me: *So what are you doing?*

Katie: *Ordering food to come here. Want to join? Mimosas at my place!!!*

I smiled at the screen and got out of bed, pulling on my maid of honor robe. I grabbed my shoes, bridesmaid dress, clutch, and jewelry before setting off to find Katie's room. I had a rough idea of which hall it was in, but I had no idea which door. Luckily, her mother Gloria was just appearing when I was taking out my phone.

"Morning, dear," she said, kissing me on the cheek. "It's the big day!"

"And it looks like the weather is perfect."

"It is. Ooh, I can't wait! I'm just going down to breakfast. Are you two coming?"

I shook my head. "Katie doesn't want to be seen until it's time for the ceremony, so she's ordering in from the kitchens."

"Very smart. I'll see you in a bit for hair and makeup." She turned to go, but I stopped her.

"Wait. Where's Katie's room?"

She pointed two doors down and I thanked her. But Katie had obviously heard our voices because I was just about to knock when it flung open, revealing her in a white-and-blue silk robe that said *Bride* on the front in cursive letters. Her face was a bright green with only her eyes and teeth showing through the goo of her facemask.

"Yay, you're here!" She grabbed my arm, pulling me in and locking the door behind me.

Her room was much the same as mine, just done up in gold and yellow with a giant pile of wrapped presents in the corner. *When Harry Met Sally* was playing on a flat screen and her dress was hanging on a hook on the wall.

"Excited?" I asked, already knowing the answer.

"Yes!" She went to the bed and hopped on.

"Did you order food already?"

She nodded and handed me a foil packet. "Yep. Now it's time for your beauty mask. You look like your skin might need a little boost."

I touched the tender skin below my eyes. "That obvious, huh?"

"No worries. Just put on the mask and the makeup team will make those bags under your eyes look designer."

I took the mask into the bathroom and tied my hair into a ponytail. My reflection peered back red and puffy. When I started smearing the green slime on my skin, it was a definite improvement.

After I washed my hands and rejoined her in the bedroom, someone knocked on the door. While Katie hid behind the wardrobe with the fear someone might see her on her wedding day looking less than spectacular, I opened it. The maid who was delivering our breakfast let out a small yelp of surprise when she saw me. But I couldn't blame her, since I knew well and good I looked like the creature from the black lagoon.

When the coast was clear, Katie was lured out from her

hiding place with the scent of bacon, eggs, toast, and hot cross buns. She laughed when she saw my face and we snapped a picture of our matching Swamp Thing looks to send to Savannah. Then we sat on her giant, four-poster bed, under the thick cover, gorging ourselves. Sure, eating so much before the wedding might have been a bad move, but in our defense, we needed the carbs to soak up the pitchers of mimosas we were inhaling. Some would call it *liquid courage*, but we just called it a basic Sunday.

A few minutes before one, Sorcha appeared, looking like she had just woken up, followed by a team of women carrying makeup cases, as well as Katie's mom. Katie and I washed off our green faces, Sorcha donned her bridesmaid robe, and the beautification began. Several stools had been brought in by the staff and the four of us were sat before the wall of windows overlooking the front of the estate.

"Is Sean's mother coming?" I asked Sorcha as my hair was wound into rollers.

She shook her head. "She isn't much for makeup and other things. But she'll come in when it's time for the final touches and all."

"She has the bridal tartan," Katie added.

Her own hair was already coming along, a pile of thick, red curls that framed her face all woven alongside a sparking headpiece.

As the afternoon wore on, we drank mimosas and talked about Katie's honeymoon to France while our faces were painted and our hair teased. I had never had professional makeup done, but when it was finished, I wished I could bring the makeup artist home with me and begin every day with the contouring, golden, glossy magic she made. I still looked like myself, only a better version with bigger eyes, clearer skin, and perfectly coated lips that pouted back at me in my reflection.

Sorcha and I slipped into our matching, light blue bridesmaid gowns while we waited for Sean's mom to show up. It was nearing three in the afternoon, time to go down and line up for the wedding. Katie was bouncing in her stool in anticipation for her final dressing. I had seen her gown when she first picked it out two months before in a fancy shop in New York City, but that was without the fittings and customization that had followed.

"Sorry I'm late." Sean's mom bustled in, a length of blue and green plaid hanging over her arm. She didn't exactly sound sorry, or look it either. I wasn't sure if her expressionless face was due to Botox, or the fact that her bun was so tight. Either way, she didn't look the least bit excited. Katie had said she was a bit of a cold fish, but I thought it was weird.

"It's alright, Carol," Katie said as she slipped from her seat and hurried into the bathroom, followed by her mother, who held a large garment bag aloft. I knew she was excited to get dressed, but she practically flew.

"Hey... so I don't know if you knew that I was on your

floor last night?" Sorcha asked quietly as we waited for Katie.

My stomach flipped. "No. But I guess you heard everything?"

"I did. I'm no' saying I'm a horrid snoop, but it's a wee bit difficult to ignore things when they're happening next to your bed and the castle is so eerily quiet at night."

The shame and embarrassment that I had pushed so far back for the day threatened to break free. "I'm sorry you had to witness all that."

"Oh, don't think of it. I only bring it up because I know what happened between Fenella and Lachlan."

"So do I," I grumbled, looking over at the empty pitcher of mimosa. I felt the need for one in that moment, but it was too late for another.

"All I'm saying is that I heard Fenella go into Lachlan's room and him kick her out a few minutes later."

"I guess it only takes a few minutes when you already know what to do."

"I don't think they *did* anything."

"So Fenella was naked and giggling for no reason?"

"How am I to know what goes through her mind? I can't tell you what she's thinking, just that she wasn't doing what you thought she was."

I raised my brows, wondering who to believe; Lachlan's cousin whom I didn't really know, or my own eyes, which clearly saw Lady Legs wrapped in the same sort of bath towel I myself had used during my own little sleepover with

Lachlan. I was about to raise that point to her when the bathroom door flew open and we all fell silent.

"Here comes the bride!" Katie's mom clapped her hands excitedly and motioned to the door.

Katie was gorgeous in a princess gown that was certainly fit for the castle. It boasted a sweetheart neckline, a ballroom skirt, and enough diamonds to put Tiffany's out of business for good. She twirled a bit, making us all *ooh* and *ahh* in honest appreciation. It was exactly what I had always pictured her getting married in. It was flashy, large, and would certainly make an entrance. Then Sean's mom draped the tartan over one shoulder, fastening it to her hip with a fancy pin.

After Gloria helped Katie into her bejeweled pumps, she passed me Katie's veil. I choked back a few tears as I carefully fastened the comb behind her tiara, leaving a cascade of fine netting trailing down her back. I wouldn't be the crybaby who sobbed all over the bride at the wedding, especially before pictures.

"I can't believe this is finally happening!" Katie said breathlessly, adjusting my pearl-drop earrings for me.

"Believe it," her mom said, looking at her watch. "We should go down, now. The florist will have all the flowers ready for us. We're making wonderful time."

Katie made me go first, to ensure that no one was left in the castle to see her, save for one of the three photographers who were documenting the wedding, and the lone florist with her box of blooms. So, when we reached the main floor, poised beside the door we would take to the aisle, the florist handed Sorcha and me small bouquets of white roses, giving a larger, fuller, version to Katie. They smelled wonderful, almost too perfect, and I wondered if they were some special Scottish version that had a hypo-scent gene.

The peppy wedding coordinator popped her head in from outside and ordered, "Mothers, come with me, please." Before saying something into her fancy little headset.

Katie's mother took one more teary-eyed look at her daughter and left the castle with a sniff, followed by Sean's silent mom. Then we took our own formation, Sorcha, me, and then Katie, who was bouncing up and down on the balls of her feet in excitement. I could hear the light sounds of a harp and the coordinator quietly counting out before saying, "Bridesmaids, go, go, *go.*"

Sorcha giggled and stepped outside, with me slightly behind. The afternoon light was blinding for a moment and I had to blink several times before I could get a good look at my surroundings. White flowers were everywhere and more lined the hedges as we reached the gardens. They were draped over bushes, tucked in pots, their petals scattered over every available surface like some sort of floral snowstorm.

I glanced back at Katie before we went into the gate and she grinned at me from behind her lacey veil. Then she pulled a ridiculous face that she quickly reined in as her dad stepped up to her side to offer her his arm. Only then could I tear my eyes away from her and begin my solemn walk towards the altar.

But just as I took the first step, Lachlan was at my side. He looped my hand through his arm and I saw in front of me, Sorcha was also paired with Richard. I had forgotten about our maid of honor and best man walk down the aisle and tried to keep my face pleasant and my eyes on the prize before me, a beaming Sean who looked fit to burst with excitement over getting married. At least someone seemed capable of keeping his attentions focused on only one woman.

As we stepped towards him, I did all I could to ignore Lachlan and focused instead on the décor. The aisle was a pristine white, lined with chairs full of men in kilts and women in large hats and the harpist struck a dramatic tune as we came into view. We were in the final stretch and I just needed to help keep the wedding on track, perfectly executed, and make sure everything stayed on the current path of beauty and refinement Katie had tried so hard to build.

Luckily, when we were stationed at the altar, I only needed to watch Katie make her grand entrance. The guests inhaled a sharp breath that was then held as she glided down the aisle. I couldn't blame them. With the sunlight raining down on her and the petals floating down from a literal drone that hovered high above, she looked like an actual fairy princess. I glanced quickly at Sean to see that he was positively brimming over with pride.

Since childhood, Katie had her wedding planned. She wanted flowers, music, a castle, and a prince to sweep her off her feet. It was like she got all of that and more. Not only was Sean her prince, he was funny, kind, supportive, and the way he looked at her made me feel completely confident he loved her with all his heart. Again, I thought to how wonderful it was they had found each other, two opposites who seemed to complement each other so well.

As the ceremony started, and I had to turn to watch the proceedings, I struggled to keep my eyes from wandering towards Lachlan. He was staring intently at me as Sean and Katie said their vows, giggling through the words. It was like he was willing me to look back. But I didn't. I kept my gaze glued to the exchanging of rings. And when it came time for the passing back of the bouquet, and Sean and Katie's mad dash to the castle, I had basically banished thoughts of him from my mind. But then I could avoid him no longer.

We stepped into the aisle and I mechanically took his proffered arm, my fingers barely touching his suit jacket. The smile I had plastered on was probably looking more like a grimace at that point, but I was determined to just keep a pleasant demeanor. I couldn't let him know how badly he had hurt me by tossing me away.

"Rose, will ye speak to me after the photographer's finished with us?" he asked through smiling teeth.

"Suck my dick, Lachlan," I replied in a sugary-sweet voice, following the wedding party and their parents towards the front of the castle.

As soon as we were out of sight of the guests, I broke away from him and settled myself beside the photographer who was tasked with taking posed pictures of us with the castle as a backdrop. That part was easy, as Lachlan and I were frequently on opposite sides of the happy couple. But then, when the family members were sent off to the party for the photographer to focus on said happy couple and their respective best friends, I could ignore Lachlan no longer.

"Now the maid of honor and best mate, aye?" the photographer called out, motioning us to the forefront of the castle.

I trudged to where Lachlan stood beside the castle's sign. I wanted to poke fun about how he was so narcissistic that his house had a giant sign with his own stupid name on it, but didn't feel like opening the lines of communication. Instead, I just stood there with a smile on my lips and my fingers clutching the bridesmaid bouquet in a death grip.

"Alright then," the photographer began, adjusting his lens and dropping to one knee. "Can you get a little closer, please?"

I took a half step nearer to Lachlan, still a bit ahead of him on the lawn so he wouldn't be in my line of sight.

"A wee bit closer?" the photographer asked again, the camera pressed to his eye. "A wee bit more... a *wee* bit more..."

We kept moving closer until my shoulder bumped

against his chest. I could feel the warmth of his body and smell the cologne he wore. With him pressed against me, it was hard to ignore I still felt some kind of sexual attraction to him. I couldn't wait until I could be dismissed and join Sorcha over at the bar. I needed to get some distance from him before it was too late. No matter how in control I thought I was, I didn't want to take a chance that some primal part of my body would take over and let him bend me over a hedge or something.

"Closer, aye? Your hand on her hip and smile!"

Click-click-click!

The feeling of his fingers brushing down my back to settle on my waist was almost too much for me to handle. His thumb rubbed over my hip bone, almost teasing me and he pulled me against him. I had to fight the urge to lean into his touch. But luckily, I didn't have to fight it too long, since Katie and Sean were sneaking off to the castle for "a celebratory glass of champagne."

As soon as the photographer lowered his camera, I was off across the lawn with Lachlan on my heels. I made a beeline for the bar beside the garden and lost him when I shimmied through a crowd of middle-aged women in giant, feathered hats. With all the guests vying to tell him how lovely his fancy castle looked, I had a fantastic barrier to shield me.

I immediately grabbed the first full glass I saw and took a long gulp. The alcohol went down smooth and I counted the hours until my plane took off—twenty-six hours and four minutes to be exact. I even thought about leaving the castle in the morning right after Katie and Sean left for France and just getting to the airport ridiculously early and sitting around in a coffee shop until boarding. Anything to get away from Lachlan.

"Ye'll be next, love," a voice said from behind me at the bar set up on the lawn.

But the voice wasn't talking to me—it was talking to Lady Legs.

Fenella was dressed to the nines in a neon pink dress that might have been cute if it wasn't probably also used as a signal flag for emergency plane landings. She also had a hat on her head, like most of the female guests. But hers had large, white flowers sticking off the side with these weird, gemstone sprigs that hung in an arch beside her chiseled cheekbone. I wondered if it was as heavy as it looked and I dearly hoped it gave her a splitting headache.

"Oh, Lady Bransen, don't jinx it!" Fenella cooed playfully. Then she added in a mock whisper, "Although, I would say to be prepared to return here *next* summer for another wedding."

I rolled my eyes and slammed my glass on the counter, ready for another... whatever the drink was. It was some specialty drink just for the wedding, the kind that was named after the bride and groom and didn't tell anyone what was in it, only that it was *Katie's Cocktail* or *Sean's Special Sip*. I had the thought that *Katie's Cocktail* was whisky-based, but I didn't really care, as long as I was drunk enough to not care about Fenella and Lachlan, but not too far gone that I would screw up my maid-of-honor speech.

I made small talk with some of the guests during the cocktail hour until it was time to go inside for dinner. The event space had been transformed overnight into a fairy forest Katie would be thrilled with. Looping ropes of vividly green ivy and white flowers were draped over candlelit tables and from the ceiling, a small band played soft music, and a low light from the chandelier helped to set the room in a warm glow. Touches of gold in the form of the cutlery added splashes of sparkle.

As I weaved through the tables, I got better looks at the centerpieces. A tall, gold vase held up bushels of white flowers that almost looked like clouds, floating above the pristine tablecloths. The roses were so pure, one might think they were fake, but every bloom was real. Sitting on loose petals were white candles in glittering holders that kept the flames just below the flowers.

I took my place at the head table beside Katie's dad. Next to him was her mother, then two empty seats for the happy couple, followed my Sean's mom, his dad... and then Lachlan. I twisted my mouth into a smile, focusing my gaze on the guests that slowly filtered in. Everyone looked around at the décor with appreciation and I hoped Katie would be just as pleased.

Suddenly loud piping music struck up and an unseen voice bellowed, "Introducing... for the first time... Mr. and Mrs. Mackinnon!"

We all stood and a trio of bagpipers entered, followed by Katie and Sean, to explosive applause. They immediately took their seats at the head table between their teary-eyed moms. I wanted to tell Katie again how beautiful she looked and how I hoped she would be happy in her new life with her new husband, but it wasn't time yet and I would be sobbing in a way that made me look so ugly, I would rival a Kardashian. And no one liked a Kardashian-style crier.

Speeches came next and a microphone appeared in my hand, given to me silently by a passing waiter. I had worked on my speech for weeks, had it all mapped out to be touching and lighthearted. There were personal stories and hilarious tales of our awkward middle school years and nostalgic bits about planning our fairy-tale weddings in my tree house. I thought I would leave people saying I gave the best speech of all time!

So, obviously, I blanked.

I stood up, suddenly aware of all the eyes that were staring at me, waiting for something profound to come out... waiting for me to talk so we could get to the dinner we could all smell from there... but I couldn't remember a single word of my speech. I was so cocky about how amazing it was and how well I could recall every line that I didn't bother to write it down. So I was left with no choice but to wing it.

"Hello everyone," I began in the soothing voice I used with all the divorcing wives at work. "It has been my honor and pleasure to be the maid of honor for Katie and Sean's big day. I've known Katie since we were in the same kindergarten class and she dumped glitter in my Hello Kitty lunchbox because I said how much I liked hers, which was covered in crystals."

There were a few laughs and I took a deep breath, feeling a little better.

"We took dance class together, had sleepovers, went to the same college, and joined the same sorority. We are as close as two friends can be... besides married ones—which are the true best friends. I can see that in Sean and Katie."

I turned to look at them and tears pricked my eyes as I spoke.

"I might have known Katie for my whole life, and only just met Sean, but I know that they're best friends. I wish you guys every happiness in the world because you both deserve it... all of it. I love you, Katie Cat."

"I love you too, Rosie Posey!" she cried in response, dabbing at her cheeks with a napkin.

Letting out a deep breath, I sank back into my chair, passing the microphone down the line. The speech turned out better than I expected. Sure, I didn't remember to include the quotes from our favorite books or talk about how we used to read bridal magazines in our dorm in college, but I thought I did pretty good. Then Lachlan gave his speech and I thought mine was complete shit.

"Love is somethin' that brings two people together, making one life out o' two. It combines, but also separates in a beautiful way. There's a before and after from that moment on, a distinct part in two lives that forever embodies what makes their past, present, and future what it was always meant to be."

He paused for a moment, the last words hanging in the air. I wondered if he had written those words or if they'd come from a book or a movie. They were so perfect and so true, total poetry. There was always a before and after when one's life had been changed. Was meeting him the beginning of my after? The time when my life was split into a world without Lachlan and the aftermath of our fleeting time together? I felt as if there might be because he had made such an imprint on my heart, I would never be the same.

I dared to glance at him. His gaze flitted away, as if he was speaking to me and not the happy couple. It was like I had caught him looking at me and he didn't have the strength to hold my stare.

He cleared his throat and began again. "This is what we all saw today—the splitting of their lives into the before and after of their journey on earth. The lives, although cut in half, are whole together, bound by the words they spoke and the rings they wear. They're bound by love and the promises that all the afters and durings and middles and beginnings of their lives will be lived together. May we all find such partnership in our own lives—the kind that Kathryn and Sean have together. *Sláinte!*"

Chapter Twelve

As soon as Lachlan had sat down, the dinner could be served. I was glad to see attention turned away from us at the head table so I could relax my stiff grin. I took a deep breath and sat back in my chair, sipping a bit of the small cups of whisky left at each seat. In fact, there were several cups of different drinks lined up in a neat row above my place. White wine, whisky, some kind of mixed drink, and champagne.

I reached for the mixed drink, but Lachlan's voice said, "Wait, Rose."

I leaned back and looked past six people to glare at him. "Excuse me?"

"Ye drink them in order with the courses, aye?"

Maintaining eye contact, I took the mixed drink and sipped it, my brow raised. If he thought he was going to tell me how to drink my alcohol, he was sorely mistaken.

He smirked in response and shook his head before moving back to his position. I did the same as waiters appeared with the first course. They bustled in like a flock of birds, pushing plates covered in delicate tops. In unison, the line broke apart and the dishes were distributed with mechanical perfection.

It was a plate with salmon and a colorful salad. I peered around as everyone began eating, taking my first bite as well. I was not a fish person, but I could have sworn it was cooked perfectly. Then I noticed everyone was drinking the glasses of fine, white wine. I took a sip and was surprised to find how perfectly it was paired with the first course. I secretly cursed Lachlan for his knowledge of all things fancy. There was nothing worse than being proved wrong, especially when the person that was right was such an asshole.

The next two courses followed swiftly; an expertly cooked steak and then a fruity sorbet I was told was there to cleanse the pallet or something else I never had to worry about in New Jersey. And the food was so delicious that by the end of it all, I was drunk on meat and seasonings and drinks and the promise of a dessert bar and the cake I helped pick out.

"Isn't it just, like, amazing?" Katie asked as she crouched down beside me on her way to the dance floor.

"Katie, it's all so gorgeous. Seriously, it's like something out of a movie."

"Now you get to see my expert dance moves."

"Are you going to tell me what your wedding song is?"

She didn't answer, just grinned and winked. That was never a good sign. The last time I had gotten that specific look was the night of our college graduation where she was part of the senior prank that included stealing a statue of Abraham Lincoln and sticking his head in the back of my Jeep because I had the top down.

The guests fell silent as Katie and Sean stepped onto the dance floor. The lights around us all grew dim and several spotlights let down a rosy glow upon the newlyweds as they took their places for their first dance. Then soft tendrils of fog wafted in from somewhere in the darkness as a small band in the corner struck the first chord.

They began a graceful waltz that took them around the dance floor in perfectly choreographed steps... to a string band rendition of the *Jurassic Park* theme song.

AN HOUR LATER, when Katie, a little bit drunk and a lotta bit loud, announced it was time for the bouquet toss, I tried to slip away unnoticed, but Sorcha was too fast for me. I had barely stood from my seat when she clamped her hand around my wrist like a vice and pulled me towards the dance floor like some manner of pushy policewoman taking me to prison.

It was filled with other single ladies, all giggling and chattering amongst themselves. Some of their boyfriends stood on the sidelines, dramatically rolling their eyes and yelling out things like "drop it, lass!" or "if she catches it, I'll have to burn the damn thing!" So, overall, the mood around us was cheerful and there was a feeling of anticipation in the air. But all I wanted to do was sink into the floor. Highlighting the fact I was still a single lady wasn't exactly something I was too keen on, especially since my separation from whatever Lachlan and I had been doing was so fresh.

"Are you ready?" Katie yelled out over her shoulder as she stood with her back to us at the edge of the dance floor. When everyone, except me, shrieked like banshees in response, she dramatically threw her bouquet over her head and into the sea of grabby hands. Mine stayed put at my side and I quickly dodged them, stepping off to the side as the roses arched through the air.

"I got it!" someone cried.

I turned to see who the lucky lady was… and *lady* it *was*. Lady Legs clutched the bouquet in her perfectly manicured fingers, grinning widely like a shark. She said something to the girl at her side and then they both looked over at Lachlan, giggling madly like a pair of braying donkeys.

"I wonder who my groom might be?" Lady Legs mused loudly as she stepped closer to Lachlan, who was looking back at her with an expression I couldn't quite place. But as soon as she laid a hand on his shoulder and held out the flowers, I was out. There was nothing more for me to see.

I whirled around, almost colliding with a large, male chest. Richard smiled down at me in pleasant surprise. I had seen him a few times since I first walked down the aisle, but hadn't spoken to him. He looked pretty handsome in his kilt and dress shirt. He had the same strong jawline all the men in the family apparently possessed and a dimpled grin I admired in his close cousin—good genes.

"No bouquet?" he asked, nodding down at my empty hands.

I shook my head, glad of his presence. It allowed me to turn away from Lady Legs and Lachlan without appearing dramatic. "I'm not a huge fan of the flower toss."

"You mean ye do no' wish to fight with a bunch o' other women for the honor and glory that comes with catchin' the bouquet?"

"Not even a little bit."

"Are ye against dancin' as well?"

"Maybe," I responded with a smile. I needed to focus my energy on someone and Richard was as good a guy as any. "Depends on who's asking."

"What if *I* asked ye?"

I shrugged. "Only one way to find out."

"Care to dance, Rose?" he asked, holding out a hand.

I nodded and he whisked me back to the dance floor, where several other couples twirled and spun to the classical covers of rock songs by the live band. His one hand settled upon my waist on the polite area that my mother would approve of. They didn't wander around like Lachlan's had in the club, although the two styles of dancing *were* wildly different. I had to wonder if I wanted Richard's hands to wander, or if them staying put exactly where they were supposed to was actually better.

I turned my head and saw Katie and Sean were there as well, but caught up in their own little world. She looked so deliriously happy and I wondered if I would ever be so content in life with a man. They were proving to be way too much trouble for me, so a life of working and solo travel with a pack of pet dogs was looking more appealing by the minute.

"Sad to leave her?" he asked, breaking my concentration on Katie and my own lackluster romantic past.

"A bit."

"I had the same troubles when I moved to Belgium for work several years ago. Starting fresh can be intimidating. Kathryn has her work cut out for her among the blue bloods, she does. Luckily, we're no' all so tightly spun."

"Are you staying in Scotland for good now?"

He shrugged a bit and I felt the movement beneath my fingers. "For the next year or so. I admit that I'm no' terribly content to stay in one place for all that long."

"It must be nice to travel for work."

"It can be. Does your work allow ye to travel much?"

"I wish! I'm firmly chained to my deck."

"Pity. I think that ye might like to see—"

"Might I cut in, Richard?" Lachlan asked beside us, smiling amiably at both of us, as if he were just swept up in the fun and romance of a wedding, instead of just flexing his muscles. I didn't think it was fair he was allowed to cavort with Lady Legs and have midnight meetings while as soon as I danced with a guy, he cut right into it. He was like a child with a toy. Even if he couldn't play with it, no one else could either.

Richard nodded. "The maid of honor and best man? O' course you shall have a round." He then backed away and nodded politely to me, saying something about him having to leave the wedding early.

My eyes widened in alarm and annoyance as Lachlan seamlessly took his place. I wanted nothing more in the world than to leave the dance floor right then and there, but the music was too low and the conversations around us too tame to allow me the privacy of bailing without some notice. Again, I was set on being the best maid of honor ever and if I needed to suck it up and be nice to Lachlan for a hot minute, then I would.

His hands began in the same spots as Richard's, although his light touch was turning out to be way more electrifying than his cousin's. I could feel his fingers through the pale blue silk covering my waist and the others were firm and warm beneath my own as he led me in an elementary form of a waltz. I tried looking away from him, but his green eyes cut into mine, holding my gaze.

"Striking up with my cousin again, aye?"

"What's it to you?"

He pulled me in closer until our chests were pressed tightly together. "I like to know what happens under my own roof."

"Don't worry, this is the last night I'll be under your roof."

"Why are ye so bitter, Rose?"

I narrowed my eyes, deliberately stomping on his foot beneath my gown. I grinned up at him as he let out a choked sound. "Oops."

"I mean it. Why are ye so vexed with me?"

"Look, I was just looking for a good time and everything, but I still don't like to see some tart in a gaudy, couture dress show me up."

He raised his brows. "This is still about Fenella?"

"Unless there's another tart in a stupid outfit strutting around and telling everyone she's the future lady of the manor, then yes, I'm talking about Fenella."

"I've told ye before, there's naught between us."

"I saw her sneaking out of your room."

"After I kicked her *out* o' my room. She snuck in when I was gettin' changed, wearin' naught but her skin."

We were drifting near the door that led out to the gardens. I could see the fairy lights through the glass of the window. "I don't care if she was in a ball gown. I don't like being made to look stupid, even though I'll never see any of these people again."

"Come on with ye, then." He moved away from me but grabbed my hand and yanked me through the door that led outside before I knew what had happened.

I tried pulling my arm away, but his hold was firm. He was marching towards the gardens, ignoring the group of older men who stood off to one side, smoking celebratory cigars. Glad to know none of them cared if some girl was about to be murdered behind a bush.

"Let go of me," I said as we became encased in the white-lit hedges. "What the hell do you think—"

His lips were on mine in a second, drowning my words. I hated to admit it, but even when I wanted to claw his eyes out, I still thought he was a fantastic kisser. But it wasn't the time for romantic princess moments where a single kiss fixed everything then all the little mice built a wedding dress from the ground up as a fairy godmother rolled a big pumpkin in from stage left and turned it into a Lamborghini. This was real life.

So I punched him in the stomach.

"Christ's blood!" He grunted, grimacing in pain. "Where did ye learn… to hit like that?"

I felt a twinge of regret, but powered through as I finally had the upper hand. Literally. "I was aiming for your dick. It's what got you in this mess in the first place."

"My cock's done nothin' to be ashamed of."

"Yeah, you would think that. You stick it everywhere!"

"I do no'." He rubbed his stomach, but stood straight. "Now, can we stop talkin' about my cock and ye can tell me what this is all about?"

"It's about you making me look stupid when you had a

girlfriend… or a friend with benefits… or whatever she is."

"She's just an old family friend and an ex."

"She seems to think there's more between you than just a shared past."

"Well there's no'. I broke up with her because she's a terrible person. She tries to get her claws back into me because o' this castle, my title, and my money."

"Doesn't she already have all that stuff on her own?"

He ran a hand through his blond hair, brushing off his forehead. "Whatever she has, I have better. Together, we would have more than a comfortable life, but I'm doin' well and good without her bleedin' me for all I'm worth."

I couldn't figure out what I thought. Did I believe him? She seemed like the kind to marry for money, but she also seemed like she could be persuasive if she wanted to. I could tell she worked out—she had the killer body to show for it.

"How am I supposed to believe that she snuck into your room in the nude and you just shrugged her off? I mean, she didn't look all that mad at being sent away."

"If she knew ye were watchin', she would no' want to seem as if she didn't get what she wanted."

"Why would she care if I saw?"

"Because she's threatened by ye."

"Threatened by *me*?" I almost laughed.

The thought that Lady Legs, with her looks, money, and apparently unlimited supply of designer goods, was in any way threatened by me, was ridiculous.

"O' course she is. She sees ye as her own competition."

"Now *that's* funny."

"No, it's true. She sees how I look at ye and it's no secret that we have somethin' more between us."

I bit my lip, unsure of how to respond. I didn't know we had *anything*, let alone something for Lady Fenella of wherever the fuck she was from to be jealous of. But I needed to know.

I had to ask. "What do we have?"

"We have a week o' good times." He took a step closer. "We have a matchin' love o' horror movies. We have the same taste in drink. We have mutual best friends who are bound together forever." Lachlan was so close, his chest nearly touched mine and one of the folds of his kilt brushed my fingertips. "And we have one more night to be together."

"Is that what you want?" I asked, my breaths coming in shallow.

"More than anythin'… granted ye do no' punch me in the gut again."

I tried to keep a straight face, but a smile broke through. "No promises."

"Well, *I* can make a promise."

"Can you?"

"I promise that I have no interest in anyone in this castle—in all of Scotland—other than *you*."

And then he kissed me.

As much as I wanted to bail on everything and drag Lachlan upstairs to get the most out of the little time we had left, it was still Katie's wedding. We went back into the castle, hand in hand, and I was pleased to see that our absence wasn't missed. We posed for a quick picture as the photographer came through and then went in for another dance. It was better than before, now that everything was out in the open and I no longer wanted to cut his dick off. I was never a great dancer, but I liked dancing more when I was with him.

It was going to make my departure for home more painful. It was terrible enough that I was going to be leaving my lifelong best friend, but now I had to say goodbye to Lachlan as well. It had been a while since I had met a guy who fit so well into the mold of what could make the perfect man. If we lived in the same city—hell, the same *country*—I thought maybe we could have had a chance at something.

"Cake, cake, cake, cake!" Katie cheered as she cut through the dance floor, Sean trailing her.

I giggled and stopped the steady rotation Lachlan and I had going. Her mood was infectious, even in the smallest doses, and we followed along with the rest of the crowd to the corner where the multitier cake was situated. I settled near the edge of the group, Lachlan's arm slung around my shoulders casually, as if it was where it was already meant to be.

The cake itself was spectacular, covered in fondant made to look like lace. It mirrored the design of Katie's opulent gown. White sugar roses and sprigs of purple heather were tucked between the layers and a large, silver letter *M* sat on top. Together, Sean and Katie picked up a silver knife and cut into the bottom tier. I waited to see if Sean would slam a piece into her face, but he didn't. I guess he valued his life because if he had gotten frosting on her gown, she might have stabbed him.

I was about to say as much to Lachlan when I saw Lady Legs watching us from the far side of the audience. While I was half-joking about Katie killing Sean, I thought it would be a distinct possibility that Lady Legs would shank me if she had a knife too. Unfortunately, her hands were hidden, so the jury was still out on if there was going to be a homicide at the wedding.

"I think I would make a good castle ghost," I muttered aloud.

Lachlan looked down at me. "What was that?"

"Oh, nothing."

"Do ye care for some dessert?"

I shook my head, one eye still on Lady Legs, who was stalking the parameter of the room like a jungle cat on the prowl. "No, I don't really like cake."

He leaned down, his lips brushing my ear. "I was no' talkin' about cake."

His words made the hairs on my arm stand on end. "I

also think there's a chocolate fountain and some scones with coffee or tea," I mentioned politely, turning to look up at him.

"There are a few things I'd like to do with chocolate, and none o' them involve being down here with an audience... unless you're into that sort o' thing?"

"Let me say good night to Katie," I whispered, spying her sneaking another glass of champagne. "I'm pretty sure they'll be heading up soon, too."

I crossed the room to where Katie and Sean stood beside the bar. His hands were roaming and I could tell by her muffled laughter that I was right in thinking she was getting ready to go up to bed just as quickly as I was.

"Heading out?" Katie asked slyly. "I see someone's made amends over there."

"Shut up."

"I can't. I'm drunk and it's my wedding. You have to indulge my every whim." Her voice dropped to a whisper. "Do you know why?"

"Because it's your wedding?"

"And because I'm a glorious princess!" she corrected, collapsing into her new husband's arms. "I'm tired."

Sean patted her back and twisted a few curls away from her face. "We'll go up now, love, will that do?"

"Mm-hm. Upstairs. Now."

"I was going to go up, too," I said, putting my arm over Katie's shoulders. "I just wanted to say good night first."

"Aw, good night, Rosie Posey!"

"Good night, Katie Cat." There were tears pricking my eyes and the same mist clouded her vision. "Shut up, Katie. Don't cry. You'll ruin your makeup."

"It's waterproof," she sobbed, falling back against Sean, who was taking it all in good humor. I was impressed. "Wake up tomorrow. Breakfast, you promise?"

"I promise."

Her face brightened and the tears disappeared at once. "Good. Now I'm gonna go consummate these nuptials with my *husband*."

"Like you didn't do that when we were all here waiting for you two to show up to the reception."

She winked at me as Sean laughed. I left her in her new husband's care. They were well suited. He seemed like the calm to her energetic fire, which I knew from personal experience was no easy task. But he seemed up to the challenge and I loved him for it. It made me feel like it would really be okay to leave her in the wilds of Scotland.

"Ready to go?" Lachlan asked as I came back to his side.

"Yeah, Katie and Sean are going up too."

"Then we—"

Lady Legs was before us then, her face a carefully composed mask. But her eyes were blazing, fueled by hellfire and sunrise Pilates. "Lachlan, where are you going?"

Lachlan sighed wearily. "Fenella... please don't do this."

"Do what, Lachlan?"

"Act like ye own me. Ever since ye came here yesterday mornin', you've givin' me nothin' but grief."

Her eyes darted towards me, but I tried to hold steady. "Lachlan," she began calmly—too calmly. "May we speak privately for a moment?"

"No."

"Now, Lachlan, I understand that some women may permit dalliances within their relationships, and I would normally be very accommodating, but I draw the line at... *this*." She motioned vaguely to me like I was some kind of modern art installment she didn't have the words for.

I should have been offended, but watching her gape at me was like watching a monstrous car wreck—I shouldn't look and I was supposed to keep on moving, but something about the wreckage waiting to explode was enthralling.

"Good night, Fenella," Lachlan asserted firmly and evenly. "And I think it's for the best that ye do no' stay here in the castle tonight. I'll have someone inform your father that ye are no longer welcome and arrange for a ride home."

Her mouth gaped for a moment and I swear I could see her brain malfunctioning like in the movie *Stepford Wives*. "Lachlan, what are you saying?"

"I'm sayin' that ye need to leave."

Her eyes narrowed and darted in my direction. "*Her* again? Are you joking?"

"Fenella, do stop before ye embarrass yourself," he said firmly under his breath.

She let out one, high-pitched laugh. "Me? Embarrass myself? You're the one who's slumming it."

Lachlan took a deep breath and placed an arm around
my shoulder. His muscles tensed as she took a step near me.
"Fenella, I will no' tell you again to leave."

Lady Legs threw down the bouquet she had been holding, scattering rose petals across the floor. Then she moved
again, bringing her hand up as if she was going to slap me.
But if there was one thing Jersey girls knew, it was how to
sidestep a bitch when they want to throw down.

I drew away from Lachlan at the last moment, allowing
Lady Legs to trip and fall down to her knees between us. She
let out a weird little screech and I noticed that many of the
guests were looking our way. Now that Katie and Sean had
left, it appeared we were prime entertainment. But although
I do love a crowd, I never did when it came to someone
causing a scene at my best friend's wedding.

I caught Sorcha's eye from across the room and tried to
telepathically plead with her for backup. As if she could read
my mind, she nodded and disappeared. In a moment, she
was beside me with a tall, thick man in a kilt and a grizzled
beard. He looked suspiciously like the same, bearded man
who graced the labels of my whisky of choice back home.

"Uncle John," Lachlan greeted the man as Lady Legs
drew herself up.

"Is everythin' alright, Lachlan?" John asked, peering at
Lady Legs distastefully.

Sorcha stepped forward and smiled sweetly up at him. "Daddy, I think Fenella had a wee bit too much to drink. Could you help her get a car back to town?"

His eyes glinted mischievously and I saw where Sorcha got her charm. "Aye, I could. Can ye walk, lass, or do ye need me to carry ye out?"

Lady Legs looked like she was about to cry and she patted her hair primly, trying to look as if she wasn't trying to attack me a few moments before. "No, I can very well walk, thank you." She tilted her head to look at Lachlan and her voice lost the razor-sharp edge. "Lachlan, may we please speak like civilized adults in private?"

"I have no more to say to ye." He shook hands with Sorcha's dad and said, "Thank ye for your help, Uncle John."

I waved at Sorcha as we turned to leave the reception. The ceremony was a beautiful success, the dinner was delicious, and the party was unforgettable. Katie had been safely and successfully married, leaving my duties as the maid of honor finished. It was like I was closing a book on our single lives together, but seeing her happy made it hurt less that I was leaving her. She would be okay and I would too.

"I'm sorry about her... about everythin'," Lachlan said as we reached the main entrance to the castle. We were the only people there. I saw as we were leaving that the other guests were in the process of saying their goodbyes, but we were still alone.

"It's okay. I was just... I don't know. These past few days

have just been so great and I guess since I'm leaving to—"

"Don't." He cut me off quickly, his fingers trailing down my arm to take my hand in his. "We still have tonight."

"Yeah, we do."

"And I intend to make the most of it."

Chapter Thirteen

I WOKE UP the next morning in a cocoon of warmth, wrapped in Lachlan's arms and the thick blankets on his bed. I didn't know what time it was, but judging by the pinkish tint of the sunlight that crept in through the gaps in the curtain, it was still early in the day.

Burrowing myself deeper into the crook of Lachlan's shoulder, I allowed myself a bit of time to wallow. There was this whole world of things in Scotland that I was going to be saying goodbye to. Katie was the top one and I could only hope to see her a few times a year at most. I would probably miss out on all the things we always said we would do together like raise our kids, travel to Italy and Spain, open up some kind of store so we could be our own bosses and hang out all the time. There were so many things I was going to miss out on.

Then there was the country of Scotland as a whole. The architecture and history were so unlike anything in New Jersey, or even the United States. And everything was done at a slower pace, allowing one to stroll down the shops and take tea at their leisure without the constant bustle of move,

move, move, *move*. Instead of dirty high-rises and highways, rolling hills and fresh air surrounded me in the Highlands.

And then there was Lachlan, although I didn't really have any right to miss him. Compared to everything else I would miss, he was brand-new, still covered in the same shiny hue all other brand-new things had. But he was more than that and I didn't want to give up the feeling I had when I was with him, the feeling we could have more than shared showers and midnight kisses, if only I had more time. But I didn't have more time. The ticket was booked and I was expected back at work in two days.

"How long have ye been up?" his low voice asked from above me, making me jump.

"What?"

"I could hear ye mumblin' to yourself."

My cheeks flushed. I hadn't thought I was talking out loud, but I was used to my solo apartment where no one was around to hear my private musings. "How much did you hear?"

"Nothin'. Ye sound like a wee mouse, all squeaky and titterin' under your breath."

"I do not," I replied, slapping him playfully on the chest.

"Mmm, ye do." He pulled me tightly to his side. "I suspect it's almost time for breakfast."

My stomach dropped as I untangled myself from him and sat up. Breakfast was the last time I would see Katie until... well, I didn't know. Months, probably. "Yeah, I guess I should probably go get ready."

"Ye mean ye do no' wish to wear the dress from last night?"

"Not really. At least let me *look* like an upstanding citizen that didn't wake up in some strange man's bed."

"I'm hardly a stranger... well, maybe just a wee bit." He propped himself on one elbow and kissed my shoulder. "Then should I come down after ye and pretend we've only just met?"

I rolled my eyes and slid out of bed. "No need to go the extra mile."

"Top drawer in the dresser. There are some shirts if ye don't wish to get all gussied up just to run down the hallway with no pants on."

"Very noble." I opened the drawer and pulled out the shirt on top. It had the logo of some random sports team on the front.

"I aim to please."

I glanced at his grinning face again as I scooped up my dress and heals from the floor and left the room. I heard voices and the sounds of morning as I scurried into my own room and locked the door behind me. If I had waited any longer, I might have been seen by my fellow early risers.

After a quick shower, in which I kept my hair dry, I put on a quick layer of makeup and brushed out the mussed curls, making them look like big, thick waves. Then I put on some leggings and an off-the-shoulder tunic. I looked pretty well rested and not at all like I had been up until five that morning finding out what a Scotsman wore under his kilt. Which, by the way, was *nothing*.

I met Lachlan in the hallway and his eyes widened in mock alarm. "Quick, hide before someone sees ye!"

I laughed and pushed him jokingly as I passed. "You're such a drama queen."

We walked down the corridor then, with him taking my hand as we went. It felt almost natural to be strolling casually through his ancestral home like that. Sure, it was cliché, but it was like I had been there more than just a few days and I belonged there just like any of the suits of armor or fancy paintings on the walls. I could see myself there with him. Only with him.

The dining room was set up for a leisurely buffet, with the long table cleared and with stations set up around the room for guests to serve themselves. I unhooked my hand from Lachlan's and took a plate, scanning the small crowd for Katie. I found her tangled up with her husband, sharing a bowl of fruit. Her eyes caught mine and she blew me a small kiss.

I grabbed some fruit and scones, as well as a large mug of coffee, and joined them at the table. Lachlan sat beside me, his own plate filled with eggs and several types of meat. Typical man.

"Hello, newlyweds," I said. "Married life looks like it suits you."

"Doesn't it just?" Katie asked as she threw her mane of curly, red hair over her shoulder. She was wearing another white dress that day, as well as a bejeweled headband that looked more like a small tiara than a casual headpiece. She was apparently milking the bride thing for all it was worth.

"Are you excited to leave for Paris?"

"Completely! Sean's been several times, so I'll have my own personal tour guide."

"Aye, Sean's very well traveled," Lachlan agreed through a bite of bacon.

"So I've heard. Anywhere you haven't been?" I asked Sean.

"Quite a few places, really. Antarctica, for one, but it's on my list."

"Why would you want to go there?"

"That's where all the penguins are, Rosie," Katie told me. Then she glanced at her watch. "Sean, the car's probably here already."

He nodded and downed the rest of his tea. "We should probably be off, then. Can't be late."

The familiar drop in my stomach was there again, a biting feeling that settled in the pit of it. This was it. This was the goodbye I knew was coming, but still could never plan for. And by the way Katie looked at me as she stood from her chair, she could feel it too. It wound around us like a fog.

"Don't go," Katie whispered as she threw her arms around me.

I laughed a little, the sound mingling with my tears. "Technically, *you're* the one leaving."

"You know what I mean. Stay—be here when I come back."

"I wish I could," I said, squeezing her tightly round the middle. "But I'll come back as soon as I can. Or you guys can visit me! You guys can take my room and I'll take the couch. I'll even get plaid bed sheets or something and leave bottles of whisky on the pillows to make you feel at home."

She giggled and pulled away, dabbing at her wet cheeks with the back of her hand. "Thank God for waterproof makeup, right?"

I nodded in agreement. "I love you, Katie. It was a beautiful wedding and you were a beautiful bride and Sean is a beautiful man and you're going to have a beautiful life."

"I love you too, Rosie. I'll send you something fabulous from France."

Then, before things got too emotional, she turned away and joined the throng of people who were setting off to the front of the castle to see them off. Lachlan was beside me, his arm around my shoulders, his hand gently rubbing it in some sort of strong, comforting way. It was nice to have him there at that moment. Saying goodbye to Katie on my own would have been too much and having someone sturdy to hold me up was apparently necessary.

There was a large, white Range Rover sitting out front in the drive. We all fanned out on either side of the stairs to get a better, final look at them. They milled through the guests, giving hugs and exchanging handshakes and kisses as they went. When they finally got to Lachlan and me, I was a mess. I'm talking ugly crying and wondering how I was going to go on type of emotions.

"Take care of her," I said to Sean as I pulled him in for a hug. "Show her Paris and Scotland and be good to her, okay? Let her eat your fries even when she said she didn't want any. And let her adopt all the dogs she wants and stick her on a plane whenever she wants."

"I will. I'll keep her safe for you and send her back as often as I can," he promised as he moved to take Lachlan's hand.

"I'm not saying goodbye," I told Katie firmly.

"Then don't," she said as she squeezed me for a fleeting moment. "I'll call you when I get back okay?"

"Okay."

Then she took Sean's hand and they turned away from us and slid into the back of the Range Rover. The back windshield said "Just Married" in neon pink paint and the driver laid on the horn as they drove off. We all stood there, waving at the car, until they disappeared around the bend in the drive.

"Ugh, that was tough," I muttered as we all began to file inside. There was a cool breeze coming in and the cheerfully sunny sky seemed to taunt me.

"Ye'll be all right." Lachlan pulled me in for a hug and I

leaned into him. "Sean's a good man and they'll come to visit ye soon enough."

"I know. It doesn't make it any easier."

"When's your flight?"

"Eight tonight."

"Only a few hours until ye leave?"

I nodded.

He pulled back. "Then care to go out with me for a bit? That is if ye do no' have other plans."

"Where to?"

"I may have set somethin' up for your final afternoon," he said slyly, nodding towards one of the footmen who seemed to always just be standing around, waiting to do shit for him. He handed Lachlan a set of car keys and he grinned down at me. "Did ye pack a pair o' sunglasses?"

><><

TEN MINUTES LATER, we were cruising down a tree-lined road in a sleek, black Mercedes convertible. The air was chilly and the wind whipped through the loose strands of hair that came out of the braid I had plaited when I saw the roofless car. But between my thick sweater and Lachlan's hand on my thigh, I could really feel the heat.

"Now will you tell me where we're going?" I asked as he turned off the main road to a narrow, recently paved lane.

"You Americans can't wait for anythin', can ye?"

"Nope," I replied, tipping down my cat-eye sunglasses to peer at him over the frames. "So spill, Braveheart, where are we going?"

He didn't answer, but picked up my hand, pressing the back of it to his lips. His mouth was cut into one of those devilish smirks that meant trouble in the best possible way. I watched him as he drove, his blond hair whipping in the wind and his strong hand gripping the wheel. He was dressed in one of the Scottish knit sweaters of his people with a pair of jeans that clung in all the right places. And every time he glanced my way, even though he wore dark glasses that only reflected myself in the lens, it was like he was undressing me with his eyes.

The road we were on was taking us farther into the line of trees we had been driving along for the first few moments of our little trip. When we had first left, I thought we were maybe going back to *The Ruins*, but it was very clear that wherever we were going, was pretty close to his house.

"There it is," he announced as the car came to a halt at the end of the short road.

All I could see was a thick forest. "What lovely... trees."

He laughed as he turned off the car and stepped into the clearing. I had just unbuckled my seat belt when he came to my side and opened the door for me. "It's beyond the trees, lass. Come."

We walked hand in hand into the tree line, following a soft path through the undergrowth that wasn't paved. I was glad I had brought boots with me for the rainy Scotland days, since the pathway wasn't exactly clear. I had to grip tightly to Lachlan for support as I stomped through the ferns and tall grass.

"Here it is," he said when we finally broke unto another clearing.

There was a squat, ancient house in the center that looked like it was straight out of a Disney movie. A steady line of smoke drifted from the chimney and the grass that surrounded it was dotted with white and yellow wild flowers. A thin, babbling stream passed by the front door and a deer hopped away as I pushed past a bush to get a better look. I half expected seven dwarves to step out on their way to a diamond mine.

"What is this place?"

"An old huntin' cabin from way back when."

"We're not hunting, are we?" I asked nervously. I was comfortable around guns and I had taken some general safety classes, but I wasn't all that keen on shooting an animal.

"No, just a wee bite and a dram." He led me towards the cabin, helping me to hop over the little brook. "If anythin' is close to real Scotland, this is it. Nature, whisky, some good food."

The old wooden front door opened with a sharp creak that told its true age. I wasn't sure what to expect when we stepped inside, but I was still pleasantly surprised. It was clean and bright, a cozy flame crackling in the large fireplace in the corner. The floors were the same worn wood as the front door and darker, open beams supported the ceiling. The walls were a pristine whitewash and beside some cabinets—obviously a newer installment—there was little inside. However, upon a table flanked by a set of chairs was a relative feast.

I took a step closer to the table, where one dish of small pastries threatened to spill out and on to the delicate, yellow tablecloth. "Wow…"

"Just a wee bite. I thought about a picnic, but that did no' go so well the last time, I felt we needed a roof in case the rain came again."

"I have to disagree with that. I remember it turning out to be a pretty nice afternoon."

He grinned. "As do I, but still, a man needs to eat and I can hardly send ye away with an empty stomach."

I looked around and spied a serving tray beneath a bowl of fresh fruit. I slid it out from beneath and began piling sandwiches, cakes, muffins, scones, chicken, fruit, and some other dishes I couldn't place. I glanced up at Lachlan, who was watching me with some interest from the doorway.

When I finished collecting the food on the tray, I pointed at it. "Take this outside."

"Ye do no' wish to eat at the table?"

"You still owe me a picnic and I plan to collect."

He laughed and deftly picked up the server, which was surprising as I thought it looked pretty heavy. But I busied myself with two crystal glasses and a decanter of amber liquid. Then I followed Lachlan back out into the sunlight.

"I do no' think there's a blanket for us to sit on."

"Afraid to get your designer jeans dirty?" I teased, sitting cross-legged on the grass beside the creek.

He rolled his eyes and sat down across from me, putting the tray between us. There weren't any plates or cutlery, so we ate with our hands, our backs being warmed by the sun. The light clouds had departed at some point during our drive and we managed to get through the picnic without being rained out again, although I wouldn't really have complained much if we had to seek shelter in that little cabin, even if it didn't have a bed.

And it turned out we didn't need one anyway, as one thing led to another and before I knew it, our afternoon picnic turned into a little afternoon delight. It was nice— lighthearted and the perfect way to work off a meal. And afterwards we dressed again and lay together in the grass, my head on his chest. I breathed him in as he ran his fingers lazily through my hair.

"I have to admit, I was pretty jealous of your toast yesterday. I had no idea you were such a romantic."

He laughed lowly. "Ach, a man can never win. Ye show her a castle, pack her a picnic, take her on a horse ride, and give her the best few rolls in the hay o' her life, and she does no' think ye a romantic until ye speak about someone else's relationship."

"Oh, stop it," I said, pressing my lips to his neck. "You know what I mean. You really must have worked hard on that. I did on mine, and look how that turned out."

"Yours was nice, very personal."

"But not as distinctly beautiful as yours."

Lachlan shrugged and I felt the movement beneath my cheek. "I just said what I thought and I hoped it would be for the best."

"I wish that kind of romance spilled into my work life like it does yours. Seeing happy couples get married at your house is going to be great."

"I hope so. History gets so lost when there's no one else to care about it."

"I say the same, exact thing! We're missing so many pieces from the greater picture just because some people didn't think it important enough to write down or turn them into verbal stories."

"That's what happened to my clan. After the Highland clearances, so many o' us lost a bit o' our history. I've collected a wee bit o' it, but research is a full-time job that I can't commit to."

I sighed, thinking to my overflowing bookcases at home. "I wish it was my full-time job. I had this friend in college who was a history major and she used to let me tag along when she went to the museums and libraries to view the collections that weren't on display. I saw so many incredible things."

"If ye love history so much, why didn't ye follow it at university?"

"Well, my parents…" I grimaced, thinking of how to explain my upbringing without sounding completely classless, then figured there was no harm in it. "My parents were broke, to say the least. My mom was a waitress on and off and when my dad was around, he would pick up construction gigs. I knew I didn't want to be like them, so I took the safe route. I was going to be a lawyer, but the extra schooling would have killed me, which is now a good thing since I don't think I could handle the workload."

"Aye, I could no' see ye as a lawyer."

"So then I became a paralegal. Got a degree in something I knew I could make money in. A degree in history doesn't have the same security. Now I have my own fun, little projects at home. I bought a few more books here to add to my collection."

"Busy lass." He ran a hand up and down my arm. "I need someone like ye on my team goin' forward. I have someone to do the work on the stone and another to keep the gardens, but I'm lackin' someone who actually cares about the history o' the place."

"I wish there was guaranteed work like that in New Jersey. I'd quit my job in a heartbeat."

There was a slight pause before he said, "Or ye could just stay in Scotland and work on Calder Castle."

Part of me wanted to accept, but just as I opened my

mouth, I realized that wasn't a job offer, it was probably just a joke. I felt silly for the momentary thought that my basic dream job was about to be given to me by the man who had given me the best sex of my life. It would have been more than lucky that I would have all that in addition to being in the same country as my best friend.

"So you know my disappointments and dreams, how about sharing a few of yours?"

"Ye ken the basic bits, the castle and the future o' openin' it. But I also own stock in a whisky company and do philanthropic work when I can. My mother had a bit o' a name when she was alive for doin' good deeds. I wanted to keep things goin' best I could."

"You've never said anything about your parents before."

"My mum was a saint o' a woman. She did no' have it in her to send me to boardin' school. She passed eight years ago and my father lives in Edinburgh now. My parents had me a bit later in life, my dad already bein' fifteen years older than my uncle John and my uncle Bruce."

"He didn't want to stay in the castle with you?"

"No' without my mother. He said the place was too big without her."

It was sweet how his parents were seemingly so in love. My own fought more than they hugged and the only time they weren't were in the few photos from my college graduation. Maybe that was why I always picked the "safe" guys, the boring ones with desk jobs, the kinds who stuck to missionary in the dark and dinner conversations about stocks and office politics. It didn't make me happy, but they were stable.

"Tell me about your philanthropy," I said, trying to urge my mind to think of other things. "What do you do?"

He opened one eye and looked at me. "Whatever I need to. I like to spread my portion from the whisky sales to whatever organization asks."

I had to admit, I was pretty impressed. Hilarious, sexy, humble, Scottish, *and* a philanthropist? It was like he was born perfect. "Very noble."

"I suppose. Do ye like livin' in America?"

"I guess. Do you like living in Scotland?"

"I guess," he countered with a grin. "I would like to visit America one day though."

I couldn't imagine why someone like him would want to leave a country so full of his own history. "You've never been?"

"Never had much o' a reason to." Lachlan then sat up and began picking some bits of leaves and grass from my hair. "But maybe I could have one now?"

"What? *Me?*"

He moved his hand to tuck a loose lock behind my ear. "Ye say that like it's a bad thing—me wishin' to visit ye and all that."

"No, I'd like that!" I blurted out, then seeing how desperate that might make me look, I said, "If you're ever in

New Jersey, I mean."

"I might find a reason to go there. Business, perhaps?"

"There aren't any clan castles on the beach," I pointed out. "Or any Scottish whisky breweries that I know about."

"I have truly enjoyed gettin' to know ye, Rose. It's just a shame I had to try that joke on your first night. We could o' had more time."

"Having more time might just make this harder," I said quietly, running my fingers over the petals of a nearby flower.

"I did no' think it would be like this either."

"And now it's over."

"Aye... but it does no' have to be, no' really."

"I live in America, you live in Scotland."

"Only a wee plane ride."

"I've seen relationships crumble when an hour separates people. And do you really want to be with someone you can only see a few times a year?"

He shrugged and the corner of his mouth lifted into a rueful smile. "Aye, I suppose no'." Then he leaned forward a little and pulled out his leather wallet. He opened it up and slid out a matte business card and handed it to me. It was velvety soft and boasted an embossed crest in one corner and all his contact printed in delicate script.

"Giving me this in case I want to make reservations at *The Ruins*?"

"I know we're leavin' things here, but if ye ever need anythin' or find yourself in Scotland and need a place to stay… give me a call or send an email and I'll see if there's any room in one o' my lavish estates."

※※

THE AFTERNOON WAS significantly colder when we left for the car and I was only too happy to press myself against Lachlan as we walked back through the forest. I snaked one hand under the hem of his sweater, letting it lie against the angle of his hip.

He pressed his lips against my hair. "Your fingers are fuckin' freezin'."

"I have anemia," I replied primly, moving to stick my other hand up his shirt as well. His muscles tensed automatically, giving me a feel of his sculpted abs.

"One o' us needs to no' die o' hypothermia."

"Then come back, or it'll be me."

Lachlan shook his head and threw his arm back around me, only letting go when we got back to the Mercedes. Thankfully, once he was inside as well, he pressed a button on the dash and the roof closed above us. But even with the heat blasting as we drove, I still shivered. It was like I wasn't capable of being warm in Scotland without Lachlan on top of me.

"Open the glove box," he ordered as he pulled the car onto the main road.

I reached down and popped it open, pulling out a length of tartan—green and blue, the colors of Lachlan's clan. "What's this?"

"A scarf for ye," he said, quickly glancing at me as he pulled to a stop to allow a sea of sheep to cross the road.

"For me?"

"Aye, I thought it'd make a good souvenir to add to your collection. After all, one o' us needed to make up for the kilt fiasco with a new bit o' tartan, aye?"

I dug into my purse and pulled out some money, and then I shoved the money into the glove box and shut the little door. "There, now we're even."

"Rose, I don't want your money."

"Well, you're driving, so you can't go searching for it. Just humor me, please?"

"Fine."

Satisfied that all debts were paid, I turned my attention to the scarf. When I unfolded it, I saw it was more like a shawl, the kind where women who wore it looked effortlessly cozy and stylish. I wasn't sure how I could pull it off, but I wrapped it around me like I had once seen a celebrity chef do at a meet and greet. "Thank you, it's amazing."

"Ye like it, then?"

"I love it," I said, fondly stroking the plaid.

He grinned at me, eyes shining with mischief. "Good. It's made from the same kilt ye murdered in cold blood."

MY BAG WAS already packed to leave, and all I needed to do was shove the rest of my toiletries and souvenirs in my extra duffel. But I was merely going through the motions, knowing I needed to leave for the airport, but not actually wanting to. I never expected it to be so hard.

"Almost ready?" Lachlan asked from the open door.

I nodded, zipping my suitcase shut. "Yep. I think that's everything."

When I turned to look at him, his mouth was set in a firm line of unhappiness. He had felt that same sparks for me that I had felt for him and me leaving would extinguish any flame between us. The fact that whatever we could have was never going to happen was really upsetting—more so than even when my only long-time ex Jake had left me while I was away for a conference. Really, I came home to an empty apartment, as he had taken all his stuff, as well as most of what we had brought together. Even that was less painful than having to say goodbye to Lachlan, especially since he hinted at doing the whole long-distance thing.

"I'll take your bag down for ye," he said evenly, picking up my suitcase and duffel while hardly looking at me.

I followed him down the stairs, my Longchamp carry-on slung over my shoulder. With each step, my heart fell a little bit more. It was my last time going down the ancient stairs, my last time passing the Calder family crest, my last time with Lachlan.

"Are ye sure I can no' drive ye?" he asked me lowly as Mattie put my suitcase in the trunk of the white Range Rover, all signs of the "Just Married" message wiped clean.

I shook my head, passing my carry-on to Mattie, who tactfully busied himself with checking the pressure on all four tires to give us some privacy. "I don't think I'd be able to say goodbye at the airport. I'd get all blotchy and wouldn't look like my passport photo, and they'd never let me on the plane."

"Ye say that like it's a bad thing."

He snaked his hands around my waist and I could feel the warmth of his palms against my back through the sweater I wore. He nuzzled his lips into my hair, holding me tightly against him. I melted in his arms, trying my hardest not to cry. I didn't want his final vision of me to be a pink, puffy, teary mess of emotions.

"I'm going to miss my flight," I said into his shirt as I breathed him in, trying to commit his scent and touch to memory.

He pulled back, nodding. "Aye, I suppose I must let ye go, then?"

"Yeah... I guess you do."

"Do no' be a stranger, Rose."

"I won't."

His eyes searched my face and he cupped my cheek with his warm hand. Then he lowered his lips to mine and kissed me. It wasn't filled with the spark of hot desire or filled with lust—it was a kiss both chaste and full of feeling. It was sweet, tasting of whisky and the berries we shared at the hunting cabin. I hated to move.

When I pulled away and opened my eyes, he was staring down at me with such intensity I had to blush. He had given me the most wild, memorable vacation imaginable and I would never forget him. But I did have to leave him and go back to reality, to meetings and paperwork and an empty apartment and weekends without Katie.

"Miss?" Mattie said after clearing his throat from behind us. "We must go now if ye want to get to the airport in time."

"I can no' convince ye to stay?" Lachlan asked quietly, touching his forehead to mine. "Just for a wee bit? A few days."

"I can't. I'd lose my job." I tried to smile and make it seem like leaving was no big deal, but I had the feeling the expression wasn't natural.

"Ye know what I want, but I agree that the distance is too hard. Ye do have a life in America."

"And you have a life in Scotland. Somebody has to keep the *Braveheart* reenactment society up and running."

That awarded me a real grin, the dimpled kind I'd grown to crave. "Aye, and I guess that's me."

"Miss," Mattie said again with a bit more force.

"Have a safe flight, Rose Hensel." His bright, green eyes

scanned my face again and he whispered, "Lord knows I'll miss ye."

He brushed his hand down my neck, his fingers combing through my hair as he dipped down to take my lips again. It was a final kiss, one that would have to be enough for the rest of our lives. I had taken the business card and said I'd keep in touch, but we both knew I couldn't. It would be torture to talk and never touch, never get back to where we were.

Then he pulled away for the last time and said, "Go now, or I'll never let ye."

Biting my lip, I stepped away, immediately feeling his absence. I wanted to say something profound and meaningful, but if I opened my mouth, I'd just cry. So I forced myself to smile and gave him a small wave as Mattie helped me in the back of the truck. Even though the windows were tinted and I was sure Lachlan couldn't see me, I kept smiling and waving pleasantly until the Range Rover had driven down the long drive and the castle was out of sight.

Only then did I allow myself to fall to pieces.

Chapter Fourteen

I SIPPED MY hot, off-brand coffee in the terminal as I waited for my flight. My suitcase and duffel were checked in baggage, my passport and ticket had been scanned, and I had just bought a new romance novel in one of the gift shops that mirrored the waiting areas. It had a hot guy on the cover and the blurb promised a college love to last and a forbidden dalliance with a British professor. I thought it nice that I could at least read about that kind of sensual life, since it wasn't like I was about to go live it.

The firm had given me an extra day off to acclimate to the five-hour time difference and get back in the swing of things. Then I was expected back in the office to deal with yet another divorcing woman trying to save her crumbling marriage while the husband was refusing alimony. I used to think I would be content with a safe career and a safe life, but I wasn't sure if I would be okay with such nothingness.

As I pondered my friendless, loveless, futureless existence in my blood-sucking career in law, I wished I had gone to one of the airport bars for a final shot of whisky. Instead, I waited for the gates to open on my flight as I clutched some black coffee that I should have honestly passed on. Luckily, I could always buy liquor on the plane, even though the travel points on my credit card wouldn't cover first class on the way back and I didn't want to splurge to cover the difference.

When the loudspeaker announced boarding for my flight, I pulled my ticket from my bag and waited my turn. As a steerage compartment rider, I had to wait for first class to board, along with people with kids, and all the rest who might need help. Then all us peasants were free to take our seats in third class like on the Titanic.

I threw out my empty coffee cup and got in line to wait for my turn. But when the woman at the desk scanned my ticket she said, "Oh, Ms. Hensel, ye've been boosted up to first class."

"I have?"

She printed something off on a little slip and stuck it to my ticket. "Yes! Enjoy your flight and thank ye for choosin' Scottish Air."

Smiling, I glanced down at my new seat number as I walked through the Jetway. It was nice and close to the front of the plane. While it wasn't going to make me going home a completely positive experience, all the champagne I could drink and a meal that wasn't vacuum-sealed slop was certainly going to help.

When I got to my chair, I couldn't believe my luck. The first seat passengers had already boarded, but the fancy little pod seat beside mine was blissfully empty, meaning I wouldn't have some weird stranger making small talk at me or judging my choice in bosom heaving literature. I could sit back with a drink and bask in all the legroom I was able to enjoy.

I had just settled myself in to my seat, snapping on the seat belt and laying out my book, headphones, and license for alcohol purchasing purchases, when my cell phone dinged. I took it as a good reminder to turn it off for takeoff when I saw the notification. I was tagged in several pictures on Facebook, all from the newlywed Katie Mackinnon's wedding album.

Since they hadn't even closed the plane doors yet, I took a moment to scroll through the pictures, my heart catching in my throat when I came to one of Lachlan and me. It was when we first stepped back into the event space after formally making up on the night of the wedding. I was looking directly into the camera, but Lachlan wasn't. His arm was around my shoulders, holding me against his side and he was gazing down at me, his dimpled smile making my stomach do flips again.

I should have left the album and turned my phone off, but I couldn't. All I had of him were a few pictures, some unforgettable memories, and part of the kilt I had "ruined" my first night in Scotland. And those jokes like, "find you a man who looks at you like you're the only girl in the world." Lachlan was looking at *me* like that and now I couldn't tear my gaze away from his stupid, handsome face.

"Good lookin' boyfriend ye've got there," said a voice from above me.

I wiped away a few tears with the sleeve of my sweater and wetly replied, "Thanks, but he's not my boyfriend."

"Would ye like him to be?"

I was about to tell the voice to shove it when I realized I *knew* that voice.

"Lachlan?" I turned slowly to look past the empty chair, where Lachlan stood in a kilt, carrying a leather carry-on in one hand and a sealed bottle of whisky in the other.

He grinned and nodded downwards. "Is this seat taken?"

Speechless, I just shook my head, wondering if I was having some weird hallucination brought on my subpar coffee.

He pushed his bag and bottle beneath the seat and sat down, leaning over the double armrest towards me. "Are ye well, lass?"

"Um... yeah. Are you really here?"

He reached out and took my hand, gently squeezing my fingers. "It appears that way."

"How—*why?*"

He held out a folded pile of bills. "I told ye payin' me back was unnecessary."

"You came all the way here to give me my money back?"

"Makes for a good excuse, aye?"

"I... what's going on?"

"I could no' let ye go like that. I know it was unfair o' me to ask ye to stay, but there was naught to say I could no' follow. I can conduct business anywhere I choose and I choose wherever in the world you are."

"So you just... booked a ticket?"

"As soon as ye drove away, I knew I made the worst decision of my life—lettin' ye go, I mean. Hell, I did no' even have your phone number and could only rely on ye decidin' to call me. I tried to wait out the feelin', to let ye go back to your real life, but it did no' work." He paused a moment, looking me over. "I knew I could never go back to my life when you were no' a part o' it."

"Then what happened?" I asked, thoroughly enthralled with his words. It was like seeing a romance novel come to life—*my* real-life romance novel.

"Well, I packed a bag as quick as I could, callin' the airlines the whole while. I managed to book two tickets in first class and then I drove like hell to the airport to make the flight."

"So you were never going to try and stop me from going home?"

"No, never. Like I said, ye have a life there, Rose. I could no' ask ye to give it up or put it in jeopardy just for a few extra days with me. It would be selfish."

"Then what are we doing, Lachlan?" I asked, my mind whirling.

He was sitting beside me, flesh and blood, following me to the United States like a backwards version of *Coming to*

America.

"I did no' come here with a ring and proposal, about to ask ye to run off with me. I came here to give us some more time—time that we deserve and time that I can no' give up. I want to give this a real try, Rose, if ye'll have me?"

"Is that really even a question?"

His expression was serious and he ran his free hand through his hair as he spoke. "Well, I did stalk your flight and follow ye upon it with no regard to what ye might want, even though ye did tell me earlier that ye wished I could come. If ye turned me down, then we'd have a long flight to suffer through. So if ye—"

I grabbed the collar of his button-down and pulled him in for a kiss. After thinking the last one I would ever share with him was the one filled with sadness from our parting, this one was absolute bliss. I was glad of the first-class privacy walls that could be raised to block out everything else. And then I wondered if all he brought with him was the little carry-on bag. I hoped he packed a suitcase as well, because now that I had him, I was never letting go.

Two Months Later

I STRETCHED LEISURELY in bed letting the last few moments of delicious sleep wash over me. The air in my bedroom was chilly with that early October feeling and I shivered a bit as I sat up. The room was still dark, thanks to my blackout shades, but the time on my phone told me it was almost noon. Even for a Sunday, that was pretty ridiculous.

There was a large T-shirt draped over the foot of the bed and I pulled it on before leaving my room. I heard the shower running as I passed the bathroom and continued on to the kitchen. There was coffee brewing, filling my apartment with the fabulous, caffeinated scent I loved. My favorite mug was even set out on the counter. It was the one I bought in Scotland, white with hand-painted purple thistles on it. I poured myself a cup and mixed in the usual cream and sugar.

When I went to put the half-and-half back in the fridge, I saw the line of postcards stuck to the face with magnets. They were all from Katie, each one outlining her honeymoon travels. There were two from Paris, one with the Eiffel Tower and a second boasting the Louvre. Another showed a castle in Avignon with *Lachlan's was better* in her flowing script on the back. But my favorite was from Versailles and had a painting of Marie Antoinette. Every time I checked my mail, I had been filled with a bittersweet feeling when I found a new postcard. Now that she was firmly settled in her new life, I was able to call, but it seemed like we always missed each other, with her hurrying off the phone the moment the pleasantries were done.

I scrolled through the emails on my phone as I sipped my coffee. I had given in my notice at the law firm, finally shedding the oppressive job of helping people untangle their marriages in divorce court. It was depressing and not at all what I wanted to do. Everything in my life had been perfectly planned, and now I was stepping into the unknown with my life packed into boxes and endless possibilities before me.

Lachlan had stayed a week with me the time he had followed me to the plane and he had come a second time for a long weekend. But he didn't just come with a bag, he had come with a job offer that I couldn't refuse. Now he was back again, helping me to pack up my life and live truly for myself.

"Rose?" Lachlan's voice called out from the bedroom.

"In the kitchen."

Lachlan appeared in the hallway, a pair of athletic shorts slung low around his hips. His hair was wet and his jaw was smoothly shaved. "Good to see ye finally up."

I rolled my eyes at him. "It's not my fault you get up at the crack of dawn to go running. Besides, you're the one who kept me up all night."

He stepped closer to me and pulled me into his chest, wrapping his arms around me. "I can no' let myself go, now that I've settled down."

"You're ridiculous."

"Ridiculously fit." He kissed the side of my head and went to fill the teakettle at the sink. "What do we have on the schedule today?"

"Nothing besides packing up a few more boxes. My cousin says she wants my office furniture, so she and her husband are going to stop by later to pick it up."

"Good. The sooner we settle affairs here, the sooner we get home."

Home. The word was so simple, but held so much meaning. We were starting a life together, building something new in Scotland, his ancestral lands that held so much adventure and history. We had inserted ourselves into each other's lives seamlessly; I had no doubt we would continue to do so.

I was going to help Lachlan rebuild his clan history from the Picts up, collecting everything I could find on Clan Calder and compiling it neatly. It was a big job, one I wasn't sure I was qualified to do, but as Lachlan had said, I had the passion for it, the drive to dig up whatever I could find. When he had offered it, I instantly had dreams of a book, pamphlets for guests, guided tours. It would be fantastic in so many ways.

"Do we have time for any fun today, or will it be all pack and work?" Lachlan asked. His kettle was set on the stove and he was standing before me, the glint in his eye told me he was up to something.

"I thought we could see a movie later on? Something scary."

His hands wandered to the hem of the shirt I wore. "I like the thought of a movie… dark, quiet… we could sit near the back."

I giggled as his fingers tickled my thigh. "Or we could stay in?"

"I think I rather like that. Order in a takeaway, see

what's on the telly…"

I melted into his arms and I had to put my mug and cell phone down. Then he placed both hands around my waist and lifted me on top of the counter, settling himself between my legs. I had once hoped that things would always be electric between us, filling me with the special brand of longing only he had been able to spark. And I hadn't been disappointed yet.

The future was full of possibilities now, the promise of adventure and love and passion like I had only thought existed in romance novels. For the first time in my life, I shed the burden of staying safe and being responsible. All it took was a hen night, a wedding, and a week in a castle to show me that what happened in the Highlands didn't always need to stay there.

The End

If you enjoyed What Happens in the Highlands,
you'll love the next book in....

The What Happens series

Book 1: *What Happens in the Highlands*

Book 2: *What Happens in the Ruins*

Book 3: Coming soon

Available now at your favorite online retailer!

More captivating reads by Tule Publishing

Beautiful Wreck by Kasey Lane

Rookie in Love by Sarah White

One More Round by Shelli Stevens

Available now at your favorite online retailer!

About the Author

From Scottish lairds to billionaire businessmen, Kelsey McKnight will ignite your soul, no matter what century it lives in.

Kelsey is a university-educated historian from southern New Jersey. She has married her great loves of romance, history, and literature to create her own tales of dashing heroes, sultry bad boys, and lovable heroines who have their own stories to tell. They will take you through the ballrooms of Victorian London, to the hills of the Scottish Highlands, and into New York City penthouses, all at the flip of a page.

When she's not writing, Kelsey can be found reading, drinking too much coffee, spending time with her family, and working for two separate nonprofit organizations.

Thank you for reading

What Happens in the Highlands

If you enjoyed this book, you can find more from all our great authors at TulePublishing.com, or from your favorite online retailer.

TULE
PUBLISHING